"There's nothing to talk about."

Claire spoke coldly. Her back was to him as she slipped into her negligee.

"All right," he said, his voice mocking. "We won't talk."

She turned, catching the intonation, but he had her in his arms before she knew it. She thrust him away, her hands violent. Nick took her shoulders in a tight grip, shaking her.

"Fight me, Claire, and you'll get hurt," he said.

"I'll divorce you," she told him.

"What grounds?" Nick asked. "Are you hoping to prove infidelity?"

"Incompatibility," she said flatly. "Breakdown of marriage."

"We're compatible, Claire. Do you want me to prove it? Given five minutes I could make you admit it." His blue eyes were challenging as they ran slowly over her.

Hating him, she knew he was right.

Other titles by

CHARLOTTE LAMB
IN HARLEQUIN PRESENTS

Other titles by

CHARLOTTE LAMB
IN HARLEQUIN ROMANCES

CHARLOTTE LAMB

the silken trap

Harlequin Books

TORONTO · LONDON · NEW YORK · AMSTERDAM
SYDNEY · HAMBURG · PARIS · STOCKHOLM

Harlequin Presents edition published August 1980
ISBN 0-373-10374-3

Original hardcover edition published in 1979
by Mills & Boon Limited

CHAPTER ONE

THEY had flown in low over a blue sea, the wingtips of the giant plane seeming almost to be about to touch the white roofs of a jagged row of skyscrapers which fringed the yellow sands before it veered sharply, losing height, circling slowly until it straightened and came down on the small airfield. Claire leaned against the window, staring out. Andrew touched her hand briefly and she turned her head to smile at him.

'Safely down,' he said, his voice amused.

She laughed. 'I'm sorry. Was my alarm that obvious?'

'You should be used to flying by now,' he told her, his brown eyes kindly. 'You've done it often enough before.'

'Yes,' she agreed, the slanting green eyes flickering away. She knew there was no point in arguing. However many times she flew she would still feel the same terror, the ache in the pit of her stomach which came from the moment she walked up the steps into the plane, the grinding agony of waiting for an expected instant of knowledge. One day, she thought grimly, it would happen. They would crash: she was convinced of it.

Andrew was watching her averted profile. She had worked for him for a year now and they knew each other very well, yet there was an enormous gap in what he knew about her of which she was aware but Andrew was

oblivious. He thought her cool, efficient and charming
—his attitude told her as much even if he had not made
it plain in words.

She turned her head again to smile at him. 'I'm fine
now,' she said lightly.

'You're very brave,' he told her in a firm voice.

She felt colour flare in her cheeks. 'I'm not!'

'Very,' he repeated, nodding. 'Only someone with
courage could face flights again and again feeling as you
do.'

It surprised her. She had not thought Andrew realised how badly she felt about flying. Embarrassed, she
unclipped her seat belt and stood up, collecting her be-
longings as the other passengers began to file past them.

As they walked into the airport lounge Claire noticed
a young soldier in Arab headdress lying full length inside a sandbagged barrier, a machine gun trained on the
airfield. Startled, she glanced round at Andrew who,
catching her glance, lifted his wide shoulders in a shrug.
'Anti-terrorists,' he muttered between tight lips.

The new glass and concrete building seemed to shim-
mer in the noon sun as they slowly passed through it,
scrutinised closely by the airport staff, their passports
studied for what seemed endless moments.

At last they took a taxi to the hotel, relaxing against
the seats, their clothes already beginning to stick to
them in the fierce heat.

'It's already changed since I was here a year ago,'
Andrew said, his brown eyes on the buildings they
passed. 'They've put up several new hotels since then.
Keravi is growing like a mushroom.'

The bright, glass palaces built to foster the new tourist trade stood out among the low, flat-topped little
houses like a sore thumb.

Much of the little port remained the same, the narrow whitewashed streets winding up the hillsides from the sea, the languorous shuffle of Arab women in their loose dark clothing, the piercing of the sky by minarets, the clouds of dust which each vehicle threw up as it swished past.

Andrew was one of the directors of a travel firm who owned shares in a new hotel at Keravi. They were hoping to put the little Arab sheikdom on the tourist map in England. The present ruler was friendly to Britain and eager to welcome British tourists. His country was tiny, largely composed of desert sands, but had a small fringe of coast to offer, an untouched area of glorious beaches and blue water which they all hoped would attract holidaymakers.

This was Andrew's first visit since he had finalised the details of the new hotel. In his absence it had been built rapidly by new building methods. As Claire stared out of the window it came into view, the white walls and high plate-glass windows glittering in the sun. It had opened at the beginning of the season, a month ago, but was only half full. Andrew wanted to check that it had been satisfactorily completed according to their specifications. Part of his job was to make sure that each hotel came up to their standards, and the local problems of the building trade had made him particularly anxious to make sure that there had been no slipshod work.

They came to a stop outside the main entrance. The flowerbeds were already neatly arranged, their colour startlingly vibrant in the bright sunshine. While Andrew spoke to the driver, Claire wandered through the doors into the carpeted foyer.

It was apparent at once that the expensive air-conditioning was working—she breathed gratefully as she felt

cool air flow over her overheated body. The reception
clerk smiled politely at her, his dark head inclined in a
bow. A few other guests standing near by watched her
walk across the floor, her long-limbed, slender body
swaying gracefully. She was wearing a classically cut
olive green suit in a lightweight material, the pleated
white jabot of her blouse flowing as she moved. Her
long black hair was swathed back from her oval face in
a carefully constructed chignon, leaving the high cheekbones and pale skin exposed. Claire was tall for her
bone structure, her body very slender. As a very young
girl she had had dreams of becoming a model, consciously learning to walk with a smooth glide which had
become second nature to her now, but somehow she
had lacked the burning ambition and tenacity necessary
for such a life, and settled for a secretarial career.

Andrew arrived, the taxi driver struggling behind
him with the luggage, and within moments they were in
the elevator on the way to their rooms. They had rooms
on different floors. Andrew had been given a large suite
on the top floor, with a terraced balcony beyond it. Claire
had a very attractive room on the floor below. Her balcony was narrow but had a striped awning over it and a
tub of flowers brightening it.

Left alone in it, she slowly stripped off and took a
lengthy shower to rid herself of the exhausting tension
of the flight. In a black towelling wrap she wandered
barefoot around the marble-floored bedroom hanging
clothes in the large wardrobe, gratefully conscious of
cool air coming into the room from the open balcony
window.

She put on a very straight, white dress, sleeveless and
simple in cut, the neckline scooped out in a boat shape,

the bodice smooth over her small, high breasts. Brushing her long hair, she piled it up on top of her head, pinning it carefully. Eyeing herself thoughtfully in the floor-length mirror, she brushed a light green eye-shadow on to her pale lids, touched her finely shaped mouth with pale pink and gently smoothed a film of pale liquid make-up into her face, giving her white skin a matt finish.

When she was ready, she turned slowly in front of the mirror, satisfied with her appearance. She was perfectly aware that part of her qualification for the job as Andrew's secretary was her faultless appearance. She enjoyed working for him, admired him and got on well with him, but she knew that he was ruthless in his attitude to those who worked for him. He expected and paid for the best—including her. If she ever fell below his standards he would sack her without hesitation. Every moment of the day and night she was on show as Andrew Knight's secretary, an extension of his own persona, and she had to be perfect.

Andrew tapped on her door a moment or two later, smiled as he glanced over her appearance, and nodded. 'You look very cool.'

'The air-conditioning works well,' she said, reminded of the fact by his remark.

'So I'd noticed,' he said, smiling. A broad-shouldered, brown-eyed, brown-haired man, he reminded her at times of a rather friendly bear, although the lightness of his manner of walking, the product of years spent in hotels, demonstrated his physical fitness and athleticism. Andrew spent hours playing badminton to keep fit.

Three days a week when he was in London he skipped lunch and spent his lunch hour in a gymnasium near by, playing squash, swimming and doing exercises. A ruggedly attractive man, a head taller than Claire, he was still a bachelor, although he had a number of women friends who visited the office from time to time, eyeing Claire suspiciously, clearly jealous of the intimacy between herself and Andrew. She often felt like reassuring them that they need not worry about her—her relationship with him was strictly a business one. She had no wish to alter its terms, and Andrew had never showed any sign of interest in her. There were ten years between them. She was just twenty-three, Andrew thirty-three. He owed his position on the board to his drive and intelligence. He owed his retention of power to his ruthless application of it. Claire knew him very well by now, but she made sure that Andrew knew very little about her. Her sense of personal privacy, her self-protective coloration demanded it.

The brown eyes glanced down at her as she walked beside him to the elevator. 'You're quite astonishing, Claire,' he said suddenly. 'Each time I see you I'm surprised at how lovely you are.'

'Thank you,' she said without emphasis, her voice quiet, faintly withdrawn. Whenever Andrew ventured too close to a personal remark she evaded him carefully.

He pressed the button and leaned against the wall, looking down into her face. 'It's odd how little I know about you despite the fact that I've known you for a year.'

'There isn't much to know,' she said calmly.

'Not even a boy-friend,' he observed lightly.

The elevator arrived and she walked into it without answering, her long, slender body upright. Andrew's eyes watched the graceful movements pleasurably. He smiled at her, his rugged face warm.

'Tell me if I'm treading on private ground,' he said, his tone slightly questioning. 'I can't believe a girl with your looks has gone unnoticed by my sex.'

She lifted the long dark lashes, her green eyes cool. 'Will you be spending the afternoon looking at the hotel?'

'Ouch,' he said under his breath, his tone rueful now. 'I take it that means the door just got slammed in my face.' His face held wry amusement. 'Yes, Claire, I'll be looking around the hotel all afternoon. And I'll want you right there with me to take notes. First we'll have a late lunch, though. The cuisine is supposed to be basically European with just the faintest flavour of Arabic cooking for those guests who like to try something different. The chef is French trained and supposed to be quite good.'

They each chose different meals to test the widest range of food possible, and on comparing notes after the meal they discovered the chef had lived up to his promise. After lunch they were taken on a tour of the hotel by the hotel manager, a French-speaking Arab with a clever, sophisticated face and sad dark eyes. His English was stiff but comprehensible.

'You need some lessons in colloquial English,' Andrew noted. 'I should see to that.'

The lightly given remark held the unspoken echo of a demand. The iron hand in the velvet glove, Claire thought drily. Typical of Andrew. He seemed satisfied, however, with what he had seen. The décor and furnishings were satisfactory, the building work up to standard. Andrew tested the sanitation, the electrical fittings, the kitchen quarters. He talked to the staff, inspected the linen, peered into cupboards and bathrooms, his eyes missing little and his brain registering everything.

By the time Claire found herself back in her own room to dress for dinner she was tired and hot, her notebook crammed with Andrew's comments in shorthand. The slightest blemish must be attended to at once—that was his way. A perfectionist, he made life difficult for those around him, and was worth his weight in gold to the company he worked for.

She joined him in the cool, tile-floored dining-room an hour later, her body smoothly encased in floating white voile printed with delicate cornflowers and trailing leaves. The low-necked bodice was supported by two white lace straps. A brief bolero of the same material covered her bare shoulders. She glanced around the room in search of Andrew and saw him talking to a little group beside the open french windows which looked out over a large swimming pool. He turned, beckoning her, a smile on his face. She crossed the room to join the group, her black head held gracefully on her long neck.

'Claire, we have a television team staying here,' he said, a spark of interest in the brown eyes. 'They're making a programme about Keravi—we'll have to look out for it back home.'

'How interesting,' she said, smiling around the little group. There were five men and one woman, although at a glance it was not easy to distinguish the woman's sex, since she wore jeans and a plain white shirt, her streaked blonde hair cut in a boyish style. Claire smiled at her and got back a friendly grin. The leonine, yellowspecked eyes flicked down over her, a rueful appreciation in the other woman's face.

'You don't look like my idea of a secretary,' said a husky voice, deep and smoky.

'She looks like mine,' Andrew said drily, his rugged face filled with amusement.

The men laughed, staring at Claire with familiar, flattering interest. Andrew began to introduce them to her, beginning with the thin Arab cameraman, his melancholy eyes feminine in their black beauty, his long hair untidily falling to his collar.

He kissed Claire's hand, a Gallic gesture which brought a hoot of derision from his friends. Andrew introduced the blonde woman last, surprising Claire, who knew his customary courtesy.

'This is Philippa Grey,' he said. 'What exactly do you do on the team, Miss Grey?'

The leonine eyes studied him. 'Research,' said the smoky voice. 'Most of it gets done back in England, but one of us always comes out with the team in case it should be necessary to dig out more details.'

'And Philippa speaks seven languages,' said the cameraman with admiration in his black eyes. 'Including Arabic.'

Claire's green eyes widened. 'Seven languages? Good heavens! You must be clever.'

'Just good at languages,' Philippa drawled, her glance flicking to Andrew's rugged face.

Claire sensed hostility between them and was not surprised. Andrew's rigid ideas of femininity would be outraged by a woman who dressed and spoke with masculine simplicity.

To avert any open trouble between them, she asked

quickly, 'And which one of you does the talking in the programme?'

'I do,' said a voice behind her.

She had turned before she had had time to think. Her oval face was pale beneath her carefully applied make-up and the green eyes widened between their dark lashes.

He was a man of catlike grace and suppleness, with a tall thin body and dark hair finely dusted with a few silver threads. From beneath heavy, cynical lids his brilliant blue eyes surveyed her in his turn. Antagonistically she was forced to admit that few women could have viewed his saturnine features with indifference. There was sensuality and power in the lines of the straight, hard mouth, chiselled strength in the strongly moulded cheekbones and jawline. He wore a dark blue shirt which was open at the throat, revealing the beginning of the dark hair on his lean chest. The casual, elegantly cut pants he wore with it were lighter in colour, a blue which almost matched the shade of the cold eyes.

Philippa moved, sliding a hand through his arm, her fingers curling on his sleeve. She smiled sideways at him. 'This is Nick Waring,' she said. 'Our talking head.'

'How do you do?' Andrew asked courteously, offering his hand.

The vivid blue eyes slowly switched from their contemplation of Claire and focused on him. 'Hi,' he drawled, shaking hands. 'You staying here?' And again the eyes flicked towards Claire. 'Or shouldn't I ask too many questions about that?'

The deliberate implication brought a flush to her cheeks. Andrew moved closer to her, his brows jerking together.

'I'm on the board of the company who own this hotel,' he said. 'And this is my secretary.' His voice had a cold ring to it, making it plain he had noted the implication behind the other man's remark.

'Oh?' The thin dark brows above the blue eyes rose. 'And you are?' The question was cool.

'Andrew Knight,' he said flatly. 'And this is Claire Thorpe, my secretary.' The second statement of that fact was meant to underline it, Claire realised.

'I'm sure you must have seen Nick on the box,' Philippa said, attempting to make peace between them, a slight bewilderment in her yellow-flecked eyes. 'He was a trouble-shooter for the news department for a few years. He's just switched to current affairs.'

Andrew contemplated him unsmilingly. 'I think the face is familiar.'

Claire licked her lips nervously. 'I think our waiter is hovering,' she said huskily. 'We'd better start dinner.'

Andrew nodded. He threw a glance around the little group. 'Nice to have met you,' he said, his eye movement deliberately not including Nick Waring. 'I hope you enjoy your stay with us.' He took Claire's slender naked arm in his hand and propelled her towards their table, his attitude one of possession. She allowed him to seat her and leaned back, her eyes on the menu, swiftly pulling a veil over the disturbed expression the last few moments had given her face.

Andrew had no intention of letting it rest there, however. He threw her a glance and muttered, 'Insolent bastard!'

She kept her eyes on the menu. 'I think I'll start with melon,' she murmured quietly. 'It's just the thing for this weather.'

'Have you ever seen him on TV?' Andrew asked, staring at her across the table.

'Yes,' Claire said flatly. 'The chicken and green peppers sounds interesting.'

'No wonder foreigners have a low opinion of English women if that blonde goes around the world in jeans and an old shirt,' Andrew said scornfully. 'She's about as feminine as one of their cameras.'

'But clever,' Claire reminded him. 'All those languages.'

'Functional, no doubt,' Andrew admitted reluctantly. 'As far as her job goes. What man would want a woman who looked and talked like a man, though?'

Claire reluctantly glanced across the room at the large table occupied by the television team. Philippa was laughing at something Nick Waring had said, her manner casually intimate, the husky voice teasing him back.

'Nick Waring seems to like her well enough,' she said coolly. 'I expect a man who roves around the world all the time appreciates her brains and courage. It takes a lot of courage to fly around with a TV team to the world's trouble spots.'

'This isn't a trouble spot,' said Andrew. 'A peaceful little oasis in the Middle East.' His brow corrugated. 'I hope it stays that way. We've invested pretty heavily over here now.'

Claire looked down at her plate. If Nick Waring was over here, trouble was bound to follow, she thought wryly, but did not say so aloud because Andrew might expect her to give some expanding remark after such a statement, and she wasn't up to it.

They ate their meal in a moody silence, neither of them seeming to have much to say. After a lengthy coffee drinking, they walked into the foyer and stood idly listening to the strong rhythmic beat of the dance band who were playing in the rectangular lounge. The tiled floor had been cleared for dancing and a few couples were moving to the music. The half empty state of the hotel had meant that the staff were especially eager to please, and waiters in white jackets and red cummerbunds were circulating around the small tables around the floor, trays of drinks in their hands.

'The band isn't bad,' she offered Andrew quietly. 'There's just a hint of Arabic music, which will probably suit most of our guests.

He nodded, his face deep in thought. 'Mmm.' After a pause he glanced at her. 'We might as well try them out.'

Surprised, she hesitated, and he stared at her, his eyes filled with a question. 'Too tired to dance?' He sounded irritable.

She smiled in resignation, knowing he would take it as a sign of failure if she admitted to weariness. They walked into the room and a waiter at once bowed them to a table. Andrew ordered a couple of drinks for them, then swept her on to the floor. He danced as lightly as if he were a boy, she thought, swaying in his strong arms. All that squash, no doubt. Her eyes lowered, amusement in them.

They returned to their table just as the TV team wandered into the room. Some of the members of it had vanished, Claire noted. The Arab cameraman caught her eye and beamed at her, walking over to speak to them. After a moment Philippa and Nick Waring joined him. Andrew gestured to the spare seats at the table. 'Have a drink,' he invited, gesturing without a pause to the waiter.

'Did you enjoy your dinner?' Claire asked the cameraman.

'Very much,' he agreed, his black eyes smiling at her. He glanced towards the band. 'They aren't bad.'

'That was what we thought,' she smiled back.

He hesitated. 'I suppose you wouldn't like to dance again?'

She laughed. 'I'd love to.' She rose and they walked on to the floor. He danced well, she decided, his movements graceful.

His black eyes inspected her oval face curiously. Well? How do my Westernised steps strike you?'

She laughed, the green eyes flicking up. 'Like the band, there's just that hint of fascinating foreign origin.'

He grinned. 'Thank you. My name is Wazi, by the way, Claire.'

He said her name with a little lilt which was entirely pleasant. 'Have you lived in England long?' she asked him.

'Since I was born,' he said teasingly.

She laughed. 'Sorry I asked!'

'Southwark,' he said. 'That's where I was born. My father was a tailor with the British army and settled in London.'

'How did you become a cameraman?'

'I was interested in photography at school,' he told her. 'I went to a big London polytechnic. I trained on cameras there and got a job in TV when I left. It's taken me eleven years to graduate to the job I've got now, and I still find cameras fascinating.'

'The eye of truth and lies,' she said dreamily.

There was a peculiar silence. Claire looked up, her oval face filled with colour, and the black eyes stared into hers with curiosity. 'That's odd—that's what Nick says. I suppose you heard him say it on television?'

'Yes,' she said, remembering the occasion. 'He was reporting from Beirut a year ago.'

Wazi nodded. 'I was there . . . it was sheer hell, believe me. You couldn't convey it through the camera lens; it's too narrow. It isn't what you show, it's what you leave out that counts.'

'Were you frightened?' she asked him, her gaze on his thin face. 'I got the impression you were all in the thick of the fighting.'

He shrugged. 'Not at the time. Later I was terrified. My wife got the worst of it. She was having a baby in London and she couldn't sleep at night for fear of what she would hear in the morning. That was why I switched from foreign reporting to home affairs. It would have broken our marriage.'

Claire nodded soberly. 'Did you mind switching?'

'It's a bit like coming off drink,' he grimaced. 'The colours are quieter and the world looks smaller and greyer, but my family came first.'

'How many children have you got?'

'Two,' he said. 'A boy and a girl.' The black eyes danced. 'I bet the team wouldn't believe it if they could hear us . . . imagine any man who was dancing with a ravishing beauty telling her about his family!'

'They're what matters to you,' she said, her face lit with a smile.

'To any man worth his salt,' he shrugged. 'We don't discuss it much in the team. I suppose Nick being a bachelor makes domestic topics taboo. He and Pippa set the pattern. We all follow.'

'She's very clever,' Claire said. 'I've no head for languages.'

'I was lucky,' Wazi shrugged again. 'I grew up speaking English and Arabic with a bit of French flung in at school. My French improved with practice as I started travelling, but I've never learnt any other languages. In most countries you can get by on some English.'

'Especially with French thrown in,' she laughed. 'Arab countries speak French rather than English, don't they?'

He nodded. The music ended and they walked back to their table. Andrew was clearly in the middle of a heated exchange with Philippa, whose square face was flushed with temper. Claire sat down and picked up her drink, her green eyes flickering from one to the other of them. Wazi sat down and lifted his own glass in a silent, amused salute, and she smiled back.

Nick Waring was leaning back in his chair, his glass in his long brown hand, his brilliant blue gaze on her. She did not look at him, but she felt the impact of his stare right through her body.

She pretended to sip her drink, her dark lashes lowered to shield her eyes, forcing herself to fight down a bitter irritation, knowing that he was perfectly aware of what he was doing.

Andrew was leaning forward in his chair, his rugged face stiff with affront. Philippa's level-headed sanity was infuriating him, Claire noted. They were discussing international politics and their views were diametrically opposed. Andrew was unused to having a woman flatly contradict him, and his brown eyes threw dislike at Philippa as he spoke loudly.

The music began again. Still concentrating on her drink, Claire was taken aback when Nick Waring got up and took it from her hand without a word.

Her green eyes flew to his face, then a hand descended on her wrist, drawing her helplessly out of her chair. She dared not protest after having danced with Wazi, so allowed him to propel her on to the dance floor without a word.

His arm came round her waist before she had time to brace herself for the intimacy of the contact. Her indrawn breath was perfectly audible, perfectly comprehended by him.

Her cheeks began to burn under his quick look. She had to allow him to take her hand into the clasp of his long fingers. Her other hand lifted as if it were made of lead and lay on his dark shoulder, trembling under the impact of the feel of his warm body under the thin cloth.

They moved away in silence. Their bodies moved as if they were long accustomed to each other, their steps flowing. Claire stared at the dark blue shirt, not daring to lift her gaze to his face. His hand tightened around her slender waist, pulling her closer, and she could not help stiffening in his arms.

'Relax,' he muttered close to her sleek hair. 'What can I do to you out here in full public view?'

Torture me, she thought wildly, and you know it perfectly well. You're enjoying yourself, you devil. Aloud she made no audible reply. The lean, tough body moving against her was draining all her energy, all her willpower. She had to concentrate on her dancing in order to force herself to forget who she was dancing with, and her nerves were beginning to affect her movement.

'So that's Andrew Knight,' he murmured sardonically. 'The hotel whizz kid. Is he your lover?'

She stared at the dark blue shirt, taking in the power of the thin muscled body beneath it with a sense of intolerable intimacy, longing for the music to end and bring the tormenting awareness of him to a conclusion.

'Cat got your tongue?' he asked mockingly, holding her far enough away to see her face.

Her lashes flickered upward reluctantly under the brilliant blue stare.

'We've got nothing to say to each other,' she said huskily.

His face lost the gleam of mocking amusement and a hard, cold expression came into it. The blue eyes shot over her oval face, lingered on the smooth curve of her pink mouth.

'I've got a lot to say to you, Claire,' he said between his teeth. 'And this time you're going to listen.'

'I've no intention of listening to a word,' she said, her face flushed.

'You'll listen if I have to tie you to a chair,' he said in a tone which barely reached her ear, his voice vibrating with temper.

'How civilised,' she retorted sweetly. 'Just what I'd expect of you. No one in the world has a right to an opinion contrary to yours, do they, Nick?'

'You don't call the mass of woolly emotions you deal in an opinion, do you?' he enquired unpleasantly.

'I'm not going to descend to an argument with you,' she threw back, trying to control her own temper.

He laughed harshly. 'That's it . . . back off as soon as you feel you might lose the battle. You're a coward, Claire.'

She flinched, but her green eyes met his directly. 'That's right,' she said tonelessly. 'At last you've got the message.'

There was a long silence while the glittering blue eyes

delved deep into her own and the hard mouth straightened. He drew a long breath and his hands tightened on her, as if defying her to try to evade him. 'But you're still my wife,' he said with a bitter little smile, 'however much you'd like to forget it.'

CHAPTER TWO

WHEN she gave him no answer, her dark lashes lowered against the smooth cheekbones, he made an irritated sound under his breath, his mouth compressed. She could feel the blue eyes probing her half averted profile, sense the tension in his lean body. The trouble was, she thought miserably, she knew him too well. They barely needed words, those clumsy instruments human beings use for communication when other channels fail. They had an almost telepathic link, forged by custom and awareness, and, try as she might, she could not entirely hide her thoughts and feelings from him, any more than he could hide his from her.

It made their present situation intolerable.

After a while, Nick said curtly, 'We're going to have to talk this out sooner or later, Claire. We're not children. For God's sake, can't we discuss it like adults?'

'There's nothing to discuss,' she said, grateful for the sudden cessation in the music. She backed away and he had to let his hands release her, although she felt in every fibre the reluctance with which he did so.

He seized her elbow to guide her back to their table, deliberately slowing her hurried escape. The dark head bent towards her and he spoke rapidly, softly, into her ear. 'I'm not putting up with it, Claire. You've got to meet me alone. And don't try to dodge it, because if you do I'll have to make the truth very clear to your boss. It's obvious he has no idea you're married, so it would be a considerable shock for him to hear about it, wouldn't it?'

She halted, glaring at him. 'That's blackmail!'

'I use whatever weapons come to hand,' Nick said, his face tight with temper. 'Anyway, why the hell shouldn't he know you're not free? You may deny me, but you can't deny our marriage. It's a legal fact and you can't push it into a cupboard and forget about it.'

Her green eyes flashed like strange jewels in their dark setting. 'I wish to God I could,' she bit out.

'Too bad,' he retorted, his strong mouth barely parting. Lines of anger and bitterness radiated from the brilliant blue eyes. 'I won't let you forget it,' he added unnecessarily.

'Yet you still masquerade as a free agent,' she pointed out in an acid tone. 'All your colleagues are unaware of our marriage, which means they still think you're a bachelor.' And still behaved like one, she thought jealously. Nick had always had a devastating effect on the women he met. She had watched at parties as his dynamic good looks and charm cut swathes through the other girls so that she could almost hear them topple helplessly at his feet as he smiled around the room, and she still found it infuriating.

His eyes narrowed speculatively on her face. 'You know why,' he pointed out. 'Did you expect me to announce our marriage after you'd walked out on me? That would have made me look a pretty fool.'

She pulled her wrist from his grasp and walked towards the table, her head high. He fell into step beside her, staring at her.

'My room number is 28,' he said softly. 'Get rid of your boss and meet me there in half an hour.'

She gave him no answer, already assuming a polite smile under the curious, interested gaze of their companions. Taking her seat, she hastily picked up her glass and took a sip, conscious of Andrew's gaze.

'Dance, Pippa?' Nick murmured, lounging casually beside the table.

Philippa gave a teasing grin. 'You must be desperate,' she said, her leonine eyes filled with laughter. 'You know I dance like an elephant with three feet!'

Nick grinned back. 'Come on, be a devil,' he said tolerantly. 'Live dangerously.'

She shrugged, rising. 'Why not? On your own head be it. I warned you!'

Claire lifted her eyes from her glass as they walked away. The friendly intimacy between them held no romantic tinge, yet she was unavoidably jealous, perhaps just because of that, since she knew Philippa shared so many things with Nick which she never could —they worked together daily in a world to which she was alien.

Putting down her glass, she hastily stood up. 'I'm tired. I think I'll turn in now.'

Andrew rose, a slight frown on his forehead. 'Early, isn't it?' He surveyed her oddly.

She met his eyes calmly. 'The flight was exhausting,' she said, no longer caring if he found such weakness irritating.

To her relief he seemed concerned rather than annoyed, however, his face serious as he surveyed her. 'I've worked you too hard in this heat,' he murmured, frowning. 'I'm sorry, Claire.'

'I'll be fine after I've had a good night's sleep,' she replied calmly. 'Goodnight, Andrew.'

For a moment she fancied he intended to go to his own room, but he hesitated, then smiled, saying easily, 'Goodnight.'

She found her way to her room, went into it and stood for a moment facing the window, the darkness enveloping her, grateful for a chance to think. The shock of seeing Nick had sent her brains into a confused tangle. She had had no time to weigh up her own reactions. Andrew's presence had meant that she had to pretend to be normal, and she had forced down the memories, emotions, fears which the sight of Nick had uncovered inside her, concentrating instead upon Andrew. Now she was alone and free to face the intolerable muddle of her own feelings.

What an ironic stroke of fate that she should find him here! She had begun to believe that she was getting over him. They had not met for over a year. At first it had been hard to stop herself constantly wanting him, longing for the sight of him. She had struggled with those emotions night after night, alone in her bed and gradually she had felt the pressure of need lessening.

She bit her lip, her arms folded across her waist to halt the shaking which was passing over her body, as if she were on the point of fever.

Whatever happened she could not let it all happen again. She had deliberately cut the threads which bound her to Nick once—she did not know if she had the strength to do so again.

Should she go to his room? She did not know if she could bear it. If she went, he would coax and bully, question and probe, until she was almost demented with the effort of retaining her ability to resist him. Nick's interrogative techniques had been learnt in a hard school. He was accustomed to much tougher opponents than herself, and she was very much afraid he would make light work of her if she allowed him the field.

But if she did not go, he would undoubtedly carry out his threat to tell Andrew the truth, and although there was no reason why Andrew should not be told she was married she knew she did not want him to hear about her marriage. He would ask questions—he was bound to. And she could not bear to talk about herself and Nick to anyone.

It was all far too complicated, far too painful, and she had hoped wildly that it was behind her for ever, when now she had to face the fact that during the past year she had merely grown a very thin skin over the bitter, torturous wound which her marriage to Nick had inflicted upon her, and today that thin skin had been wrenched away, leaving the wound exposed and aching again.

She glanced at her watch and grimaced with shock, realising that while her mind had been occupied with painful memories and hesitation about her course of action now, time had passed far more rapidly than she had imagined. She had been here for almost an hour. Nick would have been waiting for her in his room all this time, and no doubt he was by now in a difficult mood. He was not a man who liked to be crossed. He expected to get his own way, and usually did.

The first time she had met him he had been in a flaming temper because someone had attempted to thwart him—they had failed, of course, Nick had seen to that, but the battle had put him into just the right frame of mind to be furious when Claire ran hurriedly out of a shop right into him, dropping a carton of eggs during the collision, showering his elegant beige suit with broken egg. She had gasped in dismay, looking at him, stammering an apology, and felt a qualm of fear as she met the blinding, violent blue of his eyes, and heard his voice icily demand, 'Don't you ever look where you're going? What a bloody mess! You clumsy little fool!'

On the heels of fear and dismay had come a sudden outbreak of indignation. 'It was an accident,' she had flung back at him. 'I'm sorry, but you got in my way.'

He had looked so angry that she had felt her heart miss a beat. The blue eyes ran over her, narrowing. 'You got in mine,' he had said, in a changing tone. 'And I expect you to make amends for it, too. Don't think you're getting away with ruining my new suit.'

Looking at the mess she had made of the elegant garment she had felt uncomfortable and, getting out a handkerchief, began to mop up the worst of the stains, while he watched her without a word. She had been wearing old jeans, well washed to a pale blue, with an old white T-shirt which had shrunk in washing to cling to her slender body, leaving a thin line between the waistband of her jeans and her top. As it was a Saturday, she had not been working, and her hair had hung down her back in a long tail.

'There, it looks a little better,' she had muttered as she finished cleaning his suit with a furious awareness of the lean, attractive body inside it. She had not been able to ignore her own reactions as her fingers brushed against him. For the first time in her whole life she had almost felt as if her finger-ends had pulses in them which hammered as they rapidly moved against him.

Nick had silently picked up some of the scattered

groceries which still lay on the pavement around them. Claire had picked up the others, then said shyly, 'Of course, I'll pay to have your suit cleaned.'

'You certainly will,' he had replied coolly. 'You can begin by having lunch with me.'

She had blushed under the smile in the blue eyes then, making some token protest which Nick dealt with in a typical fashion by giving her a long look and saying, 'I insist,' in tones which brooked no argument. She should have been warned then, at that moment, but she had been too headily attracted to think clearly.

During that first lunch they had talked of a great many things, but for some reason Nick had suppressed all reference to his job, saying when she asked him what he did for a living, 'I'm a journalist.' Changing the subject, he had asked her about her own work, then about the girl with whom she shared an apartment. They had soon discovered a mutual passion for the cinema and spent an hour hotly arguing over old films. When lunch was over, he drove her into the country for a few hours, and they parked the car to walk across fields, following footpaths around tall, ripening barley whose whiskered ears blew rustily in the wind.

He had asked about her family as they leaned on a barred gate. Claire had been in a state of euphoric happiness by then, intoxicated by the time she had spent with him, already head over heels in love, although she had not yet admitted it to herself. She had talked eagerly about her father and her brother, Toby, who was an engineer. Her words painted for him a portrait of her home in Suffolk, the grey stone cottage, the roses and lavender which her father tended passionately every day, the cluster of apple trees and fruit bushes, the

vegetables in immaculate rows, and their excitable peki-
nese, Ling, who bit the postman and chased the birds.

'You love your home,' Nick had remarked, watching
her face. 'Why leave it for London?'

'There's very little work around in our part of Suffolk,' she had sighed. 'I go home quite often, though.'
The house and the grey sea beyond it were the back-
cloth of her life, although she did not say so to him then,
because she did not yet know him well enough to allow
him to know so much about her. The peace and permanence of the tiny village haunted her. One day she
dreamed of going back for good. London was fine, she
enjoyed her life there, but it did not satisfy her.

'Is your brother married?' he had asked, and she had
laughed.

'Toby? No. He's working on a big project in Africa,
but he's coming home in a few months.' Her eyes had
glowed. 'I've missed him.' Her voice, unknowingly, had
betrayed the understatement. Toby was one of the big
things in her life until now. As a small child she had followed him everywhere. Master, bully, protector, he had
grinned ruefully back at her tiny, plodding figure and
let her shadow him. His patience and kindness had been
rewarded with her utter loyalty.

Quietly, Nick had asked, 'And your mother?'

Her face had grown shadowed. 'Died when I was
fourteen.' Then she had quickly asked him, 'What
about your family?'

He had shrugged. 'I haven't got one. I was brought
up in an orphanage. My mother dumped me on a door-
step when I was two weeks old.'

'Oh, how terrible!' She had been shocked, looking at
him with sympathetic eyes, imagining this tall, hard

lean man as a lost small boy who had neither home nor family. No wonder he had that tough, thrusting dynamism; he must have needed it from babyhood. Pushed into an uncaring world, isolated and having to carve out his own path, he had been forged in a bitter fire.

Nick had looked down into her face curiously. 'You soon learn to survive in a hostile environment,' he had told her drily. 'I was born fighting, I think. I spent most of my boyhood doing just that, anyway. It toughens you up.'

Then he had taken her hand and turned back towards the car, and she had been so wrapped in the dizzying sensation of feeling those long, powerful fingers enclosing her own that she had forgotten everything but him, content to walk beside him in the fresh, clear air, hearing the hedges rustle with invisible birds and breathing in the sweetness of the summer afternoon.

When he asked her to have dinner with him she had not even protested at this determined take-over of her life. She had returned to her apartment, changed into a cool, strapless dress with a pleated bodice which clung to her small, high breasts, and met him again with the same eager excitement. They had dined somewhere quiet, continuing to talk, as if they each felt the same need to explore as deeply as possible the area between them. Claire had hungered to know every single thing about him: what he liked to eat, to read, to do, his favourite colours, books, music. Nothing he could have told her about himself would have failed to fascinate and intrigue her. It stunned and enchanted her that Nick seemed to feel the same way. He asked her endless questions whenever she stopped asking them of him. They poured out their thoughts and lives to each other.

Yet Claire was uneasily aware of one area of her life which she was not showing him, one deeply significant fact which she was withholding. She was tempted several times to bring it up, but each time her nerve failed her, because it was like a secret agony she could not bear to remember.

By then Nick had let drop that he worked in television news. She had been surprised and filled with admiration. 'It must be very exciting to work in television,' she had told him, and he had shrugged coolly.

'I'm used to it,' he had said.

'But you enjoy being a journalist?'

'I've always been curious,' he had admitted. 'I like to ferret out facts, and people's motives interest me. There's something about news. Once a journalist, always a journalist. However bored I get, I still feel the same prickle of excitement when a big story breaks.'

'Have you ever thought of writing a book?' she asked.

He grinned. 'Every reporter I ever met thinks about it. Few of them get around to it.'

'And you haven't?'

'I started one once when I'd had an accident and was in bed for weeks,' he said. 'I did a fantastic first chapter, then it died, and with it died my ambition to be a writer.'

He had driven her home that evening and sat in the car, his arm along the seat, looking at her intently, as if memorising her face for future reference. She had sat there, quite happy, her eyes on his, until he bent forward and at last their mouths touched for the first time. She remembered thinking that even then. The first time, she had told herself, knowing already that it would never be the last. For a few seconds the kiss had been gentle and explorative, then Nick had reached for her with those long, strong hands and she had lain in his arms, responding wildly, without hesitation, in the first exchange of deep passion she had ever experienced.

She had been kissed before and it had meant nothing. She had never known passion in her life. She knew it in Nick's arms and she returned it as hungrily as if she had been waiting for him for years.

There had been no shadow of shyness or holding back in her. None of the young men who had dated her previously would have known her. She had always been reluctant to engage in easy caresses. Prim, some of them had called her. Cold, frigid, they had muttered as they were frozen off.

Oddly, Nick had known all about that, even though she had never told him of it during their long discussions about themselves. Later, he had said wryly, 'It was obvious, my darling. You were a novice, but you learnt quickly.' Claire had laughed at that, her eyes alight. It was true. She had learnt quickly. Her inexperience had not mattered under the burning heat of her mounting desire for him. She knew that even that first night she would have put up no defence had he chosen to demand her total surrender. Her first brush with passion, and she was drowning in it already.

She was reluctant to leave him, but at last they had said goodnight, and she had stumbled into bed in a hazy dream. Next day she had waited for Nick to ring her but the call never came. Four days went by before he rang her, and by then she had died a thousand deaths. At the sound of his voice she had felt sick. Coolly she had said, 'Oh, hallo!' Nick had talked quickly, explaining that he had had an urgent call to go to Rome and had

had no chance to ring her before he left. He was at the airport now, he had said. Could he see her soon? She had begun to live again. Smiling, breathless, she had whispered, 'I'll be here.'

For a week she had seen him every evening. They had driven down to visit her father, who had taken to Nick on sight. With his usual interest in other people's lives, Nick had asked him shrewd, knowledgeable questions about his garden and Dad had answered cheerfully. 'I like him,' he had told Claire when they had a moment alone. Then he had smiled at her fondly. 'I don't need to ask if you do!'

Nick had to work hard the following week. She did not see him until the next weekend, but he had warned her about his absence and she was able to spend the time looking forward to seeing him again without feeling afraid.

He did not, she found, like talking about his job, and he never introduced her to any of his friends or colleagues. By now she knew him well enough to realise that he had a strong streak of independence in his character. He was possessive about the few things he valued in his life. 'I never share,' he had told her once, his mouth level. His years in the orphanage had taught him to guard what he owned, and that, she discovered, applied to her.

She understood, even if she did not like it, and in the beginning she loved him too helplessly to care. Had he come to her then and told her he was a bank robber, she thought, he could have got away with it. She would have forgiven him anything then.

Over the next weeks they met at irregular intervals. When Nick was in London he spent every spare moment with her. They walked, talked, went to the theatre, ate in restaurants and listened to music in his apartment. It was a tidy, spartan place, she found. Nick had left little impression on it. Even then she had thought, 'It looks as if he only visits it, not lives in it.' And she had never suspected how right she was.

One evening she became aware of a pressure within both of them which would not long be contained. Their lovemaking was growing almost desperate. 'You don't need a big wedding, do you, Claire?' he had asked abruptly. 'I don't want to cheat you of a long-cherished ambition, but for my own peace of mind I've got to marry you, and soon.'

She wouldn't have cared at that moment if he had asked her to forgo a wedding altogether. She wanted him with the same violence as he wanted her. Huskily she had told him so, and been swept into his arms, her mouth yielding under his.

'Couldn't you wait until Toby comes home?' Dad had asked plaintively, but without much hope.

Nick had looked at her coolly, his jaw tight, and she had given him a secret little smile, reading his impatience and urgency with delight.

'I'm sorry, Dad,' she had said gently, and Dad had sighed.

It had been over without fuss two days later. They spent their honeymoon at the cottage in Suffolk, at Dad's insistence, while he stayed with Aunt Joanna in Ipswich, leaving them alone during the rapturous, idyllic days and nights.

Claire's eyes closed on a long sigh. Idyllic they certainly had been, those few days before the truth broke over her unguarded head.

Then had come the phone call, and Nick's clipped, impatient voice as he explained that he had to leave her right away. There had been an earthquake in Bolivia and he had been told to catch the first flight out.

Only then had Claire begun to realise what sort of life she could look forward to, only then had she known just why the London apartment looked as if he did not live there. For a large part of the year, she found, he did not— he was abroad.

'I'm a sort of trouble-shooter,' he explained. 'I go where I'm sent at a moment's notice, usually somewhere which has just erupted into trouble. Earthquakes, crashes, revolutions . . . they're my usual fodder. I keep a bag packed at the apartment.'

'Why didn't you tell me?' she had asked very quietly, looking at her hands in her lap.

'You know why,' he had said frankly. 'You would have worried about it. It would have come between us.'

'So you married me before you let me find out,' she had said.

'I couldn't lose you,' Nick had told her, and his voice held a harsh compulsion which had sent a shiver down her back. 'I knew from the first night that my job might scare you off. You're not the type to enjoy the sort of life I lead.'

'Wouldn't you call that cheating, Nick?' she had asked him, her voice very small and clear.

He had muttered something under his breath, his manner irritable, then said flatly, 'I haven't got time to argue the rights and wrongs of it now, Claire. I have to go. Think about it while I'm away.'

Then he had walked out. The abrupt nature of the departure left her stunned. It was, she saw only too clearly, in the nature of an ultimatum. Nick had meant that she had to take him as she found him—or leave him. He had not bothered to explain, or apologise, or plead any case. He had omitted to tell her the truth because he knew from the beginning that his job would alarm her. From time to time during their courtship they had gone to parties together, and she had seen the effect he had on other women, seen the quick, assessing, interested looks he received. He was so much more experienced than she was—he must have met many women who found his roving, dangerous job exciting and glamorous. He must have guessed, too, that she was not one of them.

That first day she had laid bare her own character frankly—letting him see how much she valued permanence, stability, peace. None of these were what Nick offered her, and she had not realised it until now. She had thought that marriage would mean endless bliss. Marriage to Nick, she was forced to recognise, meant endless partings. He would never be here. He would constantly be flying away to dangerous places, leaving her behind to wait.

She had not slept at all that first night after he left. Switching on the news two nights later, she saw him giving a harrowing report from the earthquake zone. Seeing him made her cry, and knowing that he was alive made her cry again. She had already begun to dread hearing that his plane had crashed or he had caught some ghastly disease. Two days after that a second wave of quaking hit the area. She had no way of knowing whether Nick had been in the danger zone at the time, and it never occurred to her to ring and find out. She sat like a hypnotised rabbit waiting for the worst. When

Nick again appeared on her TV screen with a report she felt not relief but anger, a deep bitter anger. He had tricked her into marrying him, she told herself. Had he never suspected that his job would hurt her so much, she would not have blamed him, but he had known, and he had deliberately kept it from her as long as he could in order to make sure of her.

He was out there for two weeks. When he came home, Claire was a mere shadow of what she had been —sleepless nights had left dark rings under her eyes and lines around her mouth. She was tense, irritable, withdrawn. Nick looked at her sharply and their eyes met in a wordless knowledge.

That evening she finally told him the thing she had kept back, the story of her childhood which had been hidden. 'My father was Jimmy Brett,' she said, her eyes on her hands. 'Dad isn't my father. My mother married him when I was twelve, after my own father had been killed in that last race of his . . .'

Nick sat down heavily, his face shaken. 'Jimmy Brett . . .' He knew the name, of course. Who didn't? A brilliant, daring racing driver who won race after race in his early twenties, Jimmy Brett had had quite a following and still occasionally made the newspapers when modern drivers were compared with him and found wanting.

'My mother married him when she was eighteen. He hadn't begun to make his name then, he was just a year older. As he went on racing she got more and more afraid. He had some bad crashes, you know. Several times she thought he would be killed right in front of her eyes.' Claire sounded very cool, her voice level and indifferent. Anyone who looked closely could see, though, that her lips shook as she spoke and her skin had a peculiar pallor.

'They used to have terrible rows. I can remember listening to them and feeling terrified. Mother used to cry herself to sleep. She begged him to stop racing, but he refused. She lost a lot of weight. She was a nervous wreck by the time he was finally killed. I think it was almost a relief to her that it had happened at last—the waiting had been worse than the thing itself. Then she married Dad. She had known him before she married my father and he'd wanted to marry her then. He'd never married anyone else. He'd waited.' Claire laughed, brittle and hurt, 'Mother said Dad always guessed my father would be killed and he would get her in the end. Dad is very patient. It wasn't his idea, though, that I should take his name by deed poll, it was my mother's decision. She wanted to cut my father out of both our lives. She blamed him for it all.'

Nick was staring at her, his face set, his eyes penetrating. 'Why didn't you tell me all this before?'

'It hurt too much to talk about it,' she said bluntly. 'Mother suffered hell while my father was alive, and she made my childhood hell too. You can't watch your parents going through that sort of struggle without getting some scars yourself.'

'Then why tell me now?' he asked, knowing the answer.

'I can't take it, Nick,' she said very quietly. 'I watched my mother going through it for so long, and I want no part of it.'

'If you're asking me to change my job——' he began, and she sighed.

'I wouldn't. I know you too well.'

Nick swore under his breath. 'Look, I'm not a stupid man, or a reckless one. I value my life. I wouldn't risk it.'

'You risk it every time you go off on one of these jobs,' she said flatly, and they both knew it was true. It was what he was paid for—going out to places where life was cheap and risking getting killed just to bring back a story about it.

But Nick said harshly, 'I've been doing it for years without a scratch.'

It was not true. He had told her about 'accidents', minimising them, and suppressing the causes of them. Now she knew that he had broken limbs, been wounded by a bullet, just missed being crushed to death in Bolivia when a building fell upon his car minutes after he got out of it.

The worst of their situation was that both were so calm. They had not lost their tempers or shouted. Their voices were low and quiet, their faces were guarded.

'I could have gone while you were out there,' she said. 'I stayed to see you. But I'm going now.'

'I won't let you,' he said tersely.

'How many days in the year would you be here, Nick?' she asked. 'You would always be away.'

He lifted her from the chair and kissed her, holding her in a painful grip. Her mouth responded, her body clung. She made no effort to disguise the fact, and he lifted his head with triumph in the blue eyes. 'Claire,' he said, then the triumph died away as he saw the set of her white face.

'I couldn't take it, Nick,' she said, almost as though she begged him to understand. There was a bitter silence, then she told him what she had not yet told him, the final pain which to her made their parting inevitable. 'After she married Dad, my mother tried hard to be happy, but the scars were too serious. When I was fourteen she killed herself.'

Nick's hands dropped away from her and he stiffened. 'A bloody stupid thing to do,' he said through his tight lips. 'That must have been marvellous for you and everyone else . . . A selfish, cowardly trick for anyone to pull.'

'The years with my father had crippled her mentally,' Claire said.

'And you,' Nick muttered. 'They did you a lot of good.' His eyes flicked over her, scorn in them. 'You're a coward, Claire.'

'Yes,' she agreed levelly. 'I'm frightened of being afraid night and day the way she was . . . you have to have a strong personality to stand that sort of punishment, and I haven't got it. You knew that, Nick. That was why you hid this from me.'

They might have gone on arguing for hours if he had not got another of those phone calls. This time he was sent to Ulster, and while he was away she left him. He drove down to see Dad when he came back, but Dad had refused to give Nick her address or interfere in any way. Dad had told Claire about Nick's visit afterwards, his face sober.

'You're an adult, Claire,' he had said very gently. 'I have no intention of trying to tell you what to do, but my own opinion, for what it's worth, is that you haven't given Nick a fair chance. You loved him. You married him. Is it right to walk out on him at the first sign of a problem? Couldn't you sit down and work it out with him, darling?'

Dad had given her the only years of peace and happiness she had known. She respected and loved him. But this was something on which he could not advise her. 'I won't live in fear,' she told him frankly, 'never knowing from day to day whether or not I'll ever see him again. My nerves wouldn't stand it. I would rather cut him out of my life now. At least I won't have to wait for the phone to ring or the telegram to arrive.'

He had been silent. He remembered as well as she did what her mother had suffered and he had no easy answer to give.

Claire had reverted to her maiden name and got the job with Andrew. Nick had made no further effort to find her. That had surprised her; it had even hurt. But she had refused to let herself think about it. From time to time she had caught sight of him on the news, reporting from trouble spots around the world, but whenever he came on she turned off quickly, preferring to pretend he did not exist. Gradually she had built up a new life for herself, but she was living inside a shell, like a hermit crab, and to anaesthetise her emotions she had to discard all human contacts which might betray her into pain. Earlier boy-friends had impatiently called her cold or prim. Men she met now came up against a stone wall. She just did not want to know.

She had seen her mother torn to bits by love, and she had no intention of having it happen to herself.

She looked at her watch again. She had left it too late; Nick would not expect her now. Slowly she undressed and took a shower, then lay down on the bed, aching as though she had been through some physically exhausting trial. She knew Nick. He would ruthlessly force her to see him at some time, but she might gather enough energy to be able to face him calmly and make him leave her alone. He must have accepted their separation or he would have tried to see her long ago. They had met again purely by chance. He had to accept that. Nothing had changed.

She closed her eyes, willing sleep to arrive, but she was too worked up to sleep.

The air seemed heavy, lifeless. She turned restlessly, her hair loose around her shoulders.

It was then that she heard the tap on the door, and she sat up, trembling.

'Open the door,' Nick said quietly. 'If you don't I'll make such a racket I'll wake the whole hotel.'

'Go away, Nick! I'm too tired to argue with you.'

'Open this door and let me in,' he retorted.

'Please, Nick!'

'Do you want me to kick it down?'

He meant that. His voice was filled with burning rage. His temper was rising; Claire could feel it through the door.

Tense as a bowstring she slipped out of bed, across the room and opened the door. He pushed through it without waiting for her to open it wider than a crack, and slammed it shut behind him. She backed away, her heart in her mouth. He looked so much taller than she remembered. His face was dark with temper. His eyes moved over her in the darkness and she hurriedly turned to look for a negligee, because just that look had power to turn her body to water and she was only wearing a short cotton nightie.

'Now,' he said sharply, 'we're going to talk, Claire.'

CHAPTER THREE

WITH her back to him as she slipped into her negligee, she said coldly, 'There's nothing to talk about.'

'All right,' he said, his voice mocking, 'we won't talk.'

She turned, catching the intonation, but he was right behind her and she was in his arms before she knew it. Panic made her angry. She thrust him away, her hands violent. Nick took her shoulders in a tight grip, shaking her, his lips drawn back over the tight white teeth.

'Fight me, Claire, and you'll get hurt,' he said. 'That's a promise.'

She had to say something to stop the inevitable. Her mind worked fast, not calculating the odds carefully enough, coming up with one thing which would stop him. 'Andrew will kill you,' she said, and saw his eyes, her throat closing in alarm.

His hands tightened until they wrung a cry of pain from her. 'Go on,' he said harshly. 'You have something to tell me, I gather. I suspected as much when I saw you with him.'

'Let me go,' she said. 'You're hurting me!'

He pushed her away, his hands thrust into his dressing-gown pockets. Claire moved towards the window, her back to him, searching for the right words. She dared not make it too concrete; he might confront Andrew and that would be disastrous. She would undoubtedly lose her job and Nick would know she had lied.

'There's nothing to tell,' she said, at last. 'He doesn't

know I'm married and he thinks . . .' She let the words trail off uncertainly.

'He's your lover?' He had asked it before, not seriously, and she had not answered. Now he meant it and his voice was icy.

'Not yet,' she said, allowing him to read anything he liked into the words.

'What are you waiting for? His birthday?' Nick was using a biting tone meant to flay her.

'To be sure,' she said, turning at last to look at him in calm directness.

The blue eyes were blindingly bright. 'Sure you love him?' he asked unpleasantly. 'How long does it take? We knew the first day, didn't we, Claire?'

She winced and could not help it.

He smiled, cruelty in his face. 'What are you settling. for? Money, security, a doting husband?'

'That's my business,' she said.

'And if I refuse to divorce you?'

'I'll divorce you,' she told him. She had known she would have to do that some time, but she had never got up the courage to start the necessary procedures.

'What grounds?' Nick asked as if he were curious. 'Are you hoping to prove infidelity?'

'Incompatibility,' she said flatly. 'Breakdown of marriage.'

He laughed coldly. 'We're compatible, Claire. Do you want me to prove it? Given five minutes I could make you admit it.' The blue eyes challenged her, ran slowly over her.

'You're an attractive man,' she said, tensing but speaking calmly. 'Sexual attraction is only a small part of any relationship.'

He laughed again, his lip curling. 'Did you learn that off by heart, Claire? Trying to convince yourself of something?'

'I'm trying to convince you,' she said.

'Come to bed and try there,' he invited.

'You sound like Andrew,' she replied deliberately, and saw his eyes flash.

It was a mistake. She knew that as he crossed the space between them and took her into his arms, his hands meaning to hurt. She had made him angry when she had meant to drive him away. She had no chance of escape from him; he was too strong for her. She twisted her head away, her body struggling. Nick held her, looking down at her. She felt his stare like a brand mark, the heat of it running over her averted face, her throat, her shoulders, the tilt of her breasts. There was a long silence. She could hear his heart beating against her. Night after night she had thought of that heart ceasing to beat for ever and she had died a thousand deaths.

'This is what you're throwing away,' Nick said curtly. 'I don't even have to kiss you. We can both feel it. If I hadn't seen you for ten years it would be the same.'

'It makes no difference,' she insisted, aware that she was shaking like a leaf.

'Liar,' he told her contemptuously. 'Don't lie to me, Claire. I know.' He bent his dark head abruptly and his mouth lay against her throat, burning on her skin.

She gave a little cry, a stifled moan. She had not forgotten the pleasure of such a caress, but she had forgotten the force of it, or perhaps the year between had intensified its effect on her. She was only just hanging on to a thread of control and he had barely touched her.

'I thought you wanted to talk,' she said desperately,

throwing her head back to avoid his mouth.

He made a grim sound, half laughter, half irritation. 'Anything rather than have me touching you, Claire?'

'Yes,' she said between her teeth.

He shook her hard, his mouth taut. 'What I want from you doesn't involve talking and you know it,' he said. Then he pushed her towards the bed and she became frantic, struggling against his hands, her face white.

'Don't worry,' Nick muttered explosively. 'I've no intention of taking what you're so reluctant to give. We're going to talk. Sit down.' He almost threw her on to the bed and drew up the straight-backed little chair, facing her, his hands hanging between his knees and a fixed look on his features.

'I've changed my job,' he said brusquely.

'You're still flying into danger all the time,' she said. Ever since she knew he had left the news department she had known that he had given up doing the work he loved best, and at the back of her mind had been the suspicion that he had done it for her. It had hurt her to know that, because it made no real difference. She looked at him miserably. 'If a revolution broke out somewhere tomorrow you would be off to report it.'

'I'm not in the front line any more,' he insisted. 'I go in later when the fighting has died down.'

She looked at him levelly. 'Is that strictly true, Nick?'

He moved restlessly. 'There's a minimal risk, but no more than there would be crossing Oxford Street at the rush hour.'

She laced her fingers, looking down at them. 'Face facts, Nick. I'm not the sort of wife you need. I would have nightmares every night while you were away and when you came back I would be in such a highly strung state that we would quarrel all the time. I've lived through a marriage like that and I refuse to do it again.'

His mouth hardened. 'I don't accept that it has to be like that. You're theorising ahead of experience. Just because your parents had a bad marriage it doesn't mean we will.'

'I got a taste of it after our honeymoon,' she said. 'I went through hell when I thought you might have been killed in that second quake.'

'You shouldn't have let your imagination get the better of you,' he said impatiently.

'That's what it's all about,' she said wearily. 'I know what would happen to me and I couldn't bear it.'

'My God,' he burst out, his temper controlling him suddenly, 'why the hell did I have to fall for a cowardly little fool like you? You're spineless, Claire, a neurotic . . . you told me I'd cheated you into marriage. Maybe I did. But you cheated me. You gave me no hint of all this before our marriage.'

'I never thought it would arise,' she said in flat tones. 'I could never bring myself to talk about it all, even to you.'

'The most important part of your nature, and you hid it from me,' he said scathingly. 'I thought like a blind fool that I knew everything about you. Right from the start you seemed to be giving me the whole blueprint of your character—but you'd suppressed the vital page, hadn't you? Don't tell me it wasn't deliberate.'

'We both hid things,' she said, her eyes meeting his.

'Yes,' he said. 'I lied to get you. I would do more than that. I'd do anything I had to do, Claire. I'm warning you, if you think I've given up, you're wrong. It isn't in my character. I get what I want if I have to kill to do it.'

'Very dramatic, Nick,' she said drily. 'After a year of silence from your end, excuse me if I'm not over-impressed.'

His eyes narrowed on her face. 'Did that pique you?' A faint grin gave charm to the hard features.

'No,' she said too quickly. 'I was relieved.'

'Like hell you were,' he said lazily.

'I see. It was deliberate,' she said. That hadn't occurred to her before and she was angry to feel her senses quicken under his mocking eyes. 'How long were you intending to leave me to wonder?' she asked coldly.

'Christmas,' he said, shrugging.

She frowned, looking puzzled. 'Christmas?'

'The season of good will,' he said sardonically. 'Remember it? Your father has invited me to spend it at the cottage.'

Claire flushed angrily. 'Dad has? I don't believe it.'

'Ask him,' said Nick.

'You've been in touch with him?' Dad had never mentioned it to her, and she was shaken to think of him conspiring with Nick behind her back. She had relied upon Dad's loyalty towards her.

'I visit him now and then,' Nick told her. 'After all, he is my father-in-law.' He leaned back, his hands locked behind the dark head, his eyes moving restlessly over her. 'He gives me news of you.' He looked away, then looked back at her, his lashes flickering. 'I read your letters.'

She flushed at that. 'He had no right to let you see them!'

'Why not?' he asked sardonically. 'They never mentioned me.' His voice held bitterness. 'Not a word, not a hint. There was a great deal about Andrew Knight, though—the hotel whizz kid. Mastermind himself.'

Claire could not remember what she had written about Andrew and she felt uneasy. There would have been no hint that Andrew showed even the slightest interest in her, or that she felt anything towards him.

Nick's jaw was angular. 'I can read between the lines,' he said. 'It was obvious that Knight was interested in you. You mentioned him a damn sight too often.'

She looked away because the jealousy in his face made her heart beat too fast and she knew she couldn't hide it from him. Even so, Nick must have sensed her reaction because suddenly he was beside her on the bed and she was pinned against her pillow, his hands forceful as they held her there.

'What do you think you're doing?' she asked furiously, resisting with all her strength.

'As if you didn't know!' His voice was mocking, but there was urgency in his blue eyes as they moved over her.

She moved restlessly under their stare. Her lips involuntarily parted. Nick gave a thick exclamation, watching them, then bent the dark head and took them into his own possession with all the force of frustrated hunger.

She had told herself that she was getting over him. She had lied. She had banished Nick's image from her mind. It had haunted her sleep. Now the full weight of the long year without him broke over her, and she shook in his arms, ceasing to resist. Her hands lifted as if they had a life of their own and began to move over him, running exploringly over his powerful chest, the strong shoulders, curiously fingering his neck before they curved around it and buried themselves in the dark hair.

He freed her mouth reluctantly, his breathing fast, and looked at her in challenge. 'What else matters?' he asked her huskily, and he did not have to explain his meaning to her. 'Life is short enough anyway, Claire. Why bury yourself while you're still young? Even breathing is a risk these days, with pollution and radiation threatening the so-called civilised world. Either of us could get killed walking down a suburban street. Risk is part of being alive.'

She had had time to start thinking again, and he had lost her. She looked at him and saw the blue vein beating with life along his hard throat, and imagined his life ending on one of his trips while she was not even aware of what was happening. If she had to lose him she preferred to do it herself. It would hurt less in the long run.

'No, Nick,' she said, shaking her head.

His eyes flamed, but she had already wriggled out of his grasp while he was off guard. She rolled off the bed and stood up, tensing for a prolonged struggle. He stood up slowly and looked at her, his jaw tight.

'Very well, Claire,' he said coolly. 'A divorce, then. I'll give you all the grounds you need. I doubt if I'll have any problem finding someone to help me supply them for you.'

'I'm sure you won't,' she said, to show that he had not flicked her jealousy into bitter life at the words. Her hands curled at her sides, the nails digging into her palms.

'And if you get bored with your marriage to Knight I'll always consider an affair with you, of course,' he said bitingly. 'You're a very attractive girl, after all. As I remember it, in bed you shed most of the inhibitions which seem to bother you outside it.'

Claire walked to the door and opened it. 'Goodnight, Nick.'

He went through it like a whirlwind and she shut it after him before she broke down. She cried for a long time, lying on the bed, her sobs stifled in the pillow. When she fell asleep she was worn out.

Her alarm when it went off in the morning made her start out of sleep with a painful jerk. She switched it off fumblingly, leaning across the bed to do so, her eyes only half open. It was eight-thirty and the automatic tea machine had operated correctly. Andrew had insisted on having them installed for English visitors. She made a mental note to remark on the fact that they worked properly, then poured herself a cup of the tea, stirring milk powder into it with a grimace.

When she had drunk her tea, she wandered into the bathroom and took a quick shower before she got dressed. She had only brought two day dresses with her, as this was a brief trip, and the lemon dress she put on was one which she had had for several years. Only as she looked at herself in the mirror did she realise that it was one Nick knew; she had owned it during their days together. He had liked it, his eyes caressing whenever she wore it. The sleeves were finely pleated like a bird's wing, falling almost to her elbows. The neckline plunged in a sharp V which revealed the pale hollow between her breasts.

She bit her lip, then shrugged. Nick must make what he liked of the fact that she was wearing it today. She wasn't changing now.

Carefully she wound her black hair into its chignon, then smoothed liquid foundation into her skin before covering it with a fine coating of powder to give it a matt look. She skimmed her eyelids with a light eyeshadow and deftly outlined her mouth with pink. A touch of perfume at wrist, ears, throat and hairline and she felt armoured for any meeting with Nick.

Andrew was halfway through breakfast when she joined him. A swift, furtive glance around the room showed that there was no sign of Nick, to her relief.

Andrew's brown eyes studied her. 'You look very cool this morning,' he commented. 'How do you manage it in this climate? I feel like string.'

It surprised her. She smiled at him. 'Did you go to bed late?'

'We all stayed at the dance until late,' he agreed. 'They have stamina, those TV people. They were finishing breakfast when I got down this morning, and they've gone off to film now.'

That lifted the burden of anticipation from her, but left her feeling curiously deflated, as though the prospect of meeting Nick had lifted her spirits. She bent over her croissant, her eyes hidden.

'What are we going to do today?' she asked.

'Enjoy ourselves,' Andrew said easily.

She looked at him in surprise. It was unlike him to think of anything but work

'We'll pretend to be ordinary tourists,' he said drily, 'see what the hotel is like from the other side of the fence. You brought a bathing suit with you, I suppose?'

'Yes,' she agreed. She had hoped she would snatch time to spend a few moments in the hotel pool before they flew off again, but she had not anticipated that Andrew would suggest it; he was usually too involved in work to think of relaxation on these trips. Even his times of recreation had to have a purpose, though. In London he kept fit at the gymnasium or visited some of their London hotels for dinner or lunch. Work was never far from Andrew's mind.

He eyed her curiously. 'Does it bother you?' he asked abruptly.

'What?' Claire blinked, puzzled.

'Spending time with me when we aren't working,' he said

'Why should it?' She felt a faint flush come into her face. Since they arrived Andrew had made several remarks bordering on the personal, and it disturbed her. She did not want him to start thinking about her as anything but his quiet, efficient secretary. She had enough problems as it was.

He watched her, his brown eyes penetrating. 'Maybe I'll have a chance to find out more about you while we're here,' he said calmly.

She felt a flicker of unrest. 'There isn't anything to find out,' she said hastily.

'Your surface is very alluring,' he said, a smile on his face. 'What does it hide, though?'

She laughed, hiding her reaction of nervous dismay. 'There's only what you see,' she protested.

He looked her over, taking his time. 'As I said, very alluring,' he murmured.

Claire tightened against that look, resenting it. 'If we're going to swim I'd better change,' she said, her tone deliberately offhand.

Andrew made a face. 'It's going to be a long, hard

job,' he said with one eye on her.

She almost asked him what he meant before she caught on and her eyes flicked away from him. Andrew had never shown signs of taking an interest in her before, and she assumed that his present mood was partly induced by the heat and the holiday atmosphere. If she discouraged him firmly enough he would snap out of it. He had no real feelings towards her; it was purely a whim, this flirtatious small talk.

Getting up, she said, 'I'll go and change, then.'

Andrew got up, too, looking down at her with a glint in his brown eyes. 'We could drive around Keravi after lunch,' he said.

'Too hot,' she told him. 'They recommend a siesta, remember?'

'Why not a drive this morning, then, and a swim after lunch?' he suggested.

He was the man who paid her salary. She was here to work and she intended to make that clear. 'That's up to you,' she said coolly, her eyes distant.

He grinned, reading her expression. 'Just for today shall we forget about the office? If we're going to pretend to be holidaymakers we might as well go the whole hog.'

'You're the boss,' she said drily, her tone underlining the words.

'Not today,' he returned. 'Today I'm just Andrew . . . Claire.'

A little frown etched itself between her fine brows and unconsciously the cool oval of her face tightened into displeasure. The very last thing she wanted or needed at this moment was to have Andrew making a nuisance of himself by demanding any personal intimacy. They had always kept a distance between them until now, and she had approved of that. Why did he have to suddenly show signs of a more personal interest at this particular moment?

Briefly she wondered if he could, unconsciously, have picked up the vibrations of her emotion over Nick and misread them into something completely different. Had he imagined that she was showing signs of attraction towards him last night? But then she recalled his earlier remarks about how little he knew her. He had said that before she ran into Nick.

Her mouth compressed as she followed him out of the hotel later. One of the reasons why she had enjoyed working for Andrew during the past year had been his total indifference to her as anything but his secretary. If he began to change she would have to resign, and that would be a pity.

They drove away from the hotel in a blaze of sunshine, along a narrow street whose cobbled surface rasped the tires of the hired car, jolting them roughly to and fro between the white houses whose walls held no windows. They passed shops which sold baskets, woven chairs, objects of wood and brass and the local brand of sweet, sticky confectionery. The flood of black-garbed women and thin men in djellabahs washed over Claire's eyes. Unknowingly she was looking for Nick, who must be filming somewhere in the city, and as that fact penetrated her brain she became irritated with her own weakness. One day, and she was already aching for the sight of him. If a short time in his company could have that effect after a year apart, what chance did she have of getting him out of her bloodstream? He was like some recurring tropical disease, inescapable and sapping to the system.

Andrew wound his way through the narrow, criss-cross web of streets and came to a stop in a small square made cool by the breeze passing through palm trees which stood around a minaret-topped mosque standing behind a rough wall. A few Arab boys in stained, creased garments lay in the shade talking. They stared at the car with fascinated black eyes, pointing.

'Shall we park here and stroll around?' he asked. 'There's a market through that alley. See the stalls?'

'Why not?' Claire said vaguely, her mind still on Nick. She got out and waited while Andrew locked the car, then fell into step beside him as he moved away.

'Is there anyone, Claire?' he asked suddenly, glancing down at her.

For a full moment she stared back, bewildered by the question, then her green eyes flicked away from him and her face froze.

'You've always said that it was a mistake to mix business and pleasure, Andrew,' she told him. 'I agreed with you. I still do.'

'So mind my own business?' He sounded wry. 'I would have to be a lot less human than I am if I found it easy to pretend you were just an extension of your typewriter, you know. Is there some reason why I can't be told about your private life?'

She felt her colour rising. 'Yes,' she said tartly. 'I don't want to talk about it.'

'But you have one?' he asked persistently.

'Don't we all?'

'You know what I mean.'

'I'm not sure I do.'

'Claire, is there a man in your life?'

'Yes,' she said. 'My father. No, two—I've got a brother, too.' Her mouth twitched in sudden amusement. 'There, I've given you some information about my private life after all.'

'Very amusing,' he said without a glimmer of humour. 'You're far too attractive to have gone through life without a love affair or two. Did one of them hurt badly? Is that it?'

She was silent for a moment. They came into the market and were engulfed in the hubub of the street cries, the guttural argument of the dark-garbed women the laughter of some American tourists wreathed in cameras.

Andrew halted and turned her towards him. She looked at him with muted irritation, her oval face cool under the dark wreath of her hair.

'Still carrying a torch for someone, Claire?' he asked lightly. 'It helps to share a problem, you know.'

'There's nothing to share,' she told him flatly.

'Right,' he said, his jaw obstinate. 'Then in that case . . .' He bent swiftly and kissed her hard on her mouth. It was over before she had time to react and he walked away, leaving her with no option but to follow him, her cheeks flushed with surprise.

Andrew paused at a fruit stall, ignoring her, and concentrated on buying some oranges, using his French to bargain over them with the same tenacious determination he brought to everything he did. When he had nodded at the stallholder his shoulders were triumphant, and the man gave him a slight smile of approval as he handed the fruit over.

'Want one?' he asked Claire, offering one.

She shook her head. 'No, thank you.'

They walked around the market, drinking in the atmosphere. The heat was mounting now as the day proceeded towards noon. Andrew glanced at his watch. 'Time we got back to the hotel,' he said, slipping a hand under her elbow to turn her back in the direction of the car.

She slipped on some squashed fruit and his hand caught her back, supporting her around the waist. She straightened, trying to move away, but he held on to her.

'If we hurry we'll have time for a drink before lunch,' he said calmly.

She looked down at his hand as it lay against her waist. 'I can walk without help, Andrew,' she said, trying for a light tone.

'Are you giving me a polite "hands-off" sign, Claire?' he asked in rueful good humour.

She was on the point of replying tartly when she remembered giving Nick the idea that there was something between herself and Andrew. Her hesitation made Andrew's eyes narrow curiously on her face, watching her bite her lower lip nervously.

'Don't get the idea I'm on the point of making a violent pass at you, Claire,' he drawled easily. 'I've never been in the habit of chancing my luck with my secretaries, but is there any reason why we can't be friends?'

'No reason at all,' she said quickly.

'Then try smiling at me as if you don't hate the sight of me, will you?' he asked in light tones, but with a faint soberness in his brown eyes.

'Is that how I smile at you?' she asked lightly. 'As if I hate the sight of you? I'm sure I don't.'

'This morning it's been like going for a drive with Lady Macbeth,' he nodded. 'I've been waiting for the dagger in my back.'

She laughed. 'You're exaggerating.'

'Only just,' he grimaced.

'It must be the heat,' she shrugged.

'Oh, is that all?' He did not sound convinced, but he was apparently ready to accept her word for it. They walked and his arm stayed around her waist without any protest from her, although she was very relieved when they reached the car and he had to remove it. They drove back along the maze of narrow little streets, jolting to and fro on the cobbles, and arrived back at the hotel just as a van was unloading the television equipment under Wazi's wary eye. He saw her and grinned, waving a hand, and Claire smiled back at him cheerfully.

Andrew parked the car and Claire got out and stood beside it, waiting for him. Her ear suddenly picked up the approaching resonance of a familiar voice. It sent a quiver of response through her veins just to hear it at a distance, and she was so filled with self-derision at her own weakness that as Andrew joined her she deliberately turned a brilliant smile upon him, seeing his blink of surprise as their eyes met.

'When you smile like that, Claire, you're quite something,' he murmured to her, bending his head as if he was about to kiss her.

'Am I?' she asked softly, her head tilted back a little, the green eyes clear and smiling.

He stared, as if taken aback by her sudden encouragement. 'But you're a puzzle,' he said under his breath. Then a grin twisted his mouth. 'A very attractive one, though,' he added, curving an arm around her waist and turning her towards the hotel. She did not look round to see if Nick had noticed Andrew's proprietorial arm around her. She did not need to. Nick was walking right behind them and she could feel the intensity of his stare right through her back.

CHAPTER FOUR

WHEN they had been briefly to their rooms to wash, they met again downstairs in the bar. Andrew was already there when Claire walked into the room. He was seated at a table around which sat most of the TV team and she heard his voice raised impatiently, so that she was not surprised to find him arguing with Philippa again. There was a flush on Andrew's belligerent face, a sparkle in his eyes. He was so intent on what he was saying that he did not even notice as Claire walked up to them. Nick saw her as soon as she walked in—his eyes had been fixed on the door, as if he had been waiting for her to appear. She tilted her head, keeping her eyes on the others, so that he might not think she was aware of his gaze, even though every fibre of her being was stretched to resist the heady delight of feeling those blue eyes move over her.

He didn't get up as she reached the table. She stood beside Andrew, laying a hand on his shoulder to let him know she had arrived. He did not pause in his assertive remarks to Philippa, but he half turned his head with a quick smile, putting his own hand over hers to hold it against his shirt.

He had changed before he came down and was wearing a chocolate shade of shirt with casual beige pants. The outfit made him look less the tycoon/whizz kid and more as if he fitted the company he was keeping. Philippa was looking at him warily, running a hand through her short streaky hair.

'That's all very well,' she said as he paused at last. 'But what you're saying leaves out the human element.'

'The provision of work in under-developed countries can hardly be said to do that,' he retorted, his jaw jutting.

'Come on!' Philippa snapped. 'The high moral tone sounds great, but it's the profit motive that interests you.'

Andrew said, 'Thanks!' After a tight pause he turned and smiled warmly at Claire, indicating the chair next to him. 'What will you have to drink? The usual?'

It made it sound as if they drank together all the time, when in fact they almost never did, but she played up to it coolly. 'Yes, thanks.'

He snapped a finger and thumb without looking round and the barman materialised smoothly. Everyone in the hotel knew who Andrew was, and he got the service he expected.

Claire smiled around the table, not quite reaching Nick. 'Have a good morning?'

'Great,' Philippa said drily. 'Everywhere we went we met a great big nasty brick wall. Nobody was talking to us today. We used up some film on local street scenes and that was it.'

'Perhaps you have as much charm for them as for me,' Andrew said.

There was an uncomfortable silence. Nick leaned forward, one long hand flat on the table, and said in a soft voice, 'Are you asking to get your face pushed through the back of your head?'

Andrew wasn't taking that from anyone. He turned, bristling, his eyes ready for trouble. Claire put her hand over his arm, squeezing it. He looked down quickly at her and she shook her head at him in silent appeal.

Huskily, she said, 'Perhaps you haven't bribed the right people, Philippa,' and laughed at her pleadingly.

Philippa was ready to co-operate in making the peace. She laughed back, shaking her head. 'Maybe that's it,' she pretended to agree. She glanced over Claire's dress, sighed. 'Every time I see you, you look fantastic. How do you do it? That dress has Bond Street stamped all over it.'

Claire shook her head smilingly. 'Try Oxford Street,' she told her. 'A big chain store, and it was very reasonably priced. I can't afford Bond Street prices on my salary.'

Andrew must be feeling edgy, she thought, as he reacted at once. 'Your salary is pretty good for a secretary,' he said, turning to look reproachfully at her, as though she were accusing him of penny-pinching.

Nick was turning his glass in his hand, his eyes on it, and she risked a quick glance at him. His pale grey shirt was unbuttoned half the way to his waist. Against the soft shade he looked very bronzed, his skin glowing with vitality. While her eyes were lingering on him he looked up, as if he felt her glance, and their eyes collided. Claire felt her face burn as if she had been caught doing something betraying, which in fact she had, of course, because he knew her too well not to know exactly what she had been thinking, feeling, as she stared at the hard brown chest left bare by his open shirt.

The waiter distracted attention from her by delicately placing her drink in front of her, giving her the opportunity of fiddling with the glass; lifting it to her lips and sipping it slowly.

Wazi was talking cheerfully about the film he had taken that morning. 'Good colour stuff,' he said, shrugging. 'Those market shots will cut in well.'

Philippa leaned over to speak to Nick confidentially, lowering her voice, and he inclined his head with a smile to listen to her murmured remarks.

'Feeling hungry yet?' Andrew asked Claire, laying an arm casually about her shoulders, his brown eyes smiling into her face.

'It's too hot to feel really hungry,' she shrugged. 'But I suppose we might as well try to eat something.'

Nick flickered a glance at them, observing Andrew's arm around her with dangerous blue eyes which came back to her face, narrowed and hostile.

She lowered her lashes while she finished her drink and put the glass down on the table. 'Ready,' she told Andrew smilingly.

He looked round at the others. 'We'll see you, then,' he said. 'We're planning to relax around the pool after lunch. Too hot to do anything else.'

'I shall do what all sensible Arabs do,' said Wazi, grinning. 'Sleep all afternoon.'

'Why don't we make up a party for dinner?' Andrew asked casually. 'On the house, of course.'

'I bet your expenses are more generous than ours,' Wazi groaned. 'Thanks, we'd like that. Wouldn't we?' Looking round the table at the rest of the team he raised an eyebrow.

The others all looked at Philippa, which wasn't surprising, since whenever she and Andrew were within speaking distance of each other they burst into bitter argument. They were like strange dogs who bark wildly whenever they meet. It was a form of territorial instinct,

Claire imagined; each was defending their own strip of personal territory.

Andrew's skin flushed slightly. He looked at Philippa, too, his expression guarded. She gave him a long, thoughtful look, then shrugged. 'Why not?' she said off-handedly.

The others relaxed. The sound recordist grinned. 'The least we'll expect is champagne, I warn you,' he told Andrew.

'Champagne it is,' Andrew grinned. 'I'll order it in advance, then it will be at the right temperature. We have quite a good cellar, actually. It's just been stocked, of course.'

'You're making me feel thirsty,' said Wazi, laughing.

'You always feel thirsty,' Philippa teased him.

He leaned over the table and lifted her hand to his lips, his eyes filled with amusement. 'Lady, you're so right,' he agreed.

'Coming?' asked Andrew, taking Claire's hand in a tight grip. She looked at him in surprise and nodded, following him.

'They get on well together, all of them,' she remarked as they went through into the dining-room.

'God knows why,' he said irritably. 'That woman is enough to drive any man mad. You only have to open your mouth to have her jump down your throat. I've never met a woman who argues so much!'

Claire looked at him curiously. 'You might try humouring her,' she suggested, tongue in cheek.

He lifted his head belligerently. 'Why the hell should I? I've got a right to my own opinions and a right to express them.'

'So has she,' Claire pointed out.

'Do you agree with her?' He looked offended. Andrew always had to be right. He could not tolerate opposition. He steamrollered over it if he could.

Claire smiled. 'I may not agree with her, but I'd fight to the death for her right to have an opinion and express it,' she said. 'Just as I would for you in the same circumstances.'

'Fair enough,' he retorted, glaring at her over the top of the menu. 'But does she have to be so dogmatic about everything?'

She smothered another smile. He had no sense of humour where his own views were concerned. 'Maybe you should just avoid controversial subjects?' she suggested.

'And what?' He looked sarcastically at her. 'Talk about the weather and the score in the latest cricket match?'

Her green eyes filled with laughter. 'Why not, if it keeps the peace? Unless,' she added, slyly, 'you actually enjoy arguing with her.'

'Enjoy it?' Andrew sounded as though she had insulted him. He glared at her. 'What sane man would? After talking to her for five minutes I feel as though I've done three rounds with the world heavyweight champion!'

The waiter appeared, hovering deferentially. They ordered and sat back, watching as the TV team filed into the room, their voices blending cheerfully. Philippa was walking with Nick, laughing at something he had just said. He did not glance towards Claire, all his attention fixed on Philippa, and as they reached their table he ushered her forward, a long brown hand on her back.

'Look at the clothes she's wearing now,' Andrew muttered, his eyes on them. 'Those everlasting jeans get shabbier every time I see them and her shirt looks as though she's slept in it.'

'Maybe she's wise to dress so casually,' Claire proposed lightly, 'travelling around with a bunch of men as she does.'

'Camouflage, you mean?' He stared at the blonde head as it moved to smile at Nick. 'Why bother? Who would bother her even if she wore a bikini?'

'I think she's attractive, in her way,' Claire said. Firmly she added, 'And I like her.' Even if she did share Nick's life day in, day out, facing danger with him fearlessly, talking to him on equal terms, her manner infuriatingly familiar.

Andrew turned and gave her a quick, searching look, then smiled in sudden warmth. 'She was right about one thing, anyway. That dress is fantastic.'

'Thank you,' she said. 'Every compliment is welcome.'

'I'd like that in writing,' he retorted. 'Every time I've tried to compliment you in the past you've given me the big freeze.'

She had meant it as a joke, but she was grateful to him for getting her through the minefield of being under the same roof as Nick for a few days, so she smiled at him.

'That was when we were secretary and boss,' she reminded him. 'For today we agreed to be on holiday.'

'And that makes things different?' He watched her, leaning back casually in his chair, a large, broad-shouldered, powerful man with an aggressive thrust to his chin. Claire felt a quiver of uneasiness. It might not be a sensible idea; to give Andrew the impression that she was encouraging him to pay her attentions. He was not the sort of man with whom one could get involved safely on any casual basis. He expected to have his own way in any relationship, and although if he himself had no serious intentions, he might make a pleasant occasional companion, if for any reason he chose to make demands, he would be a difficult opponent if one refused him.

She had hesitated long enough to sharpen the glance he was resting on her face. She shrugged lightly, trying to make a joke out of her reply. 'It lessens the danger.'

'Of what?' he asked at once.

'Of mixing business with pleasure,' she said, still making it into something to laugh about.

'Meaning that once we go back to normal, the compliments have to stop?'

'Well, in the nature of things,' she said helplessly.

'Yes?' He raised an eyebrow, eyeing her, forcing her to put it into words.

Claire was relieved that at that moment their first course arrived, followed at once by their wine. It left her free to pretend to be absorbed by her food while Andrew tasted the wine and nodded curtly to the wine waiter. By the time they were alone again, the topic had been safely shelved, and she was able to launch into a neutral subject, her manner cool.

When they had finished lunch they went upstairs, talking easily. Andrew seemed to have shed his irritable humour. He was laughing at an anecdote she told him about her brother Toby.

'So he's an engineer? Travel much?'

'Quite a bit since he qualified.'

'He's older than you?'

'Two years,' she admitted.

'Are you close?'

'Very,' she agreed, her tone soft as she thought about Toby. They had grown closer than ever after their mother died. The shock had been worse for Toby than for her, Claire often thought. He had been in a difficult phase, having problems adjusting to Dad after having adored their father with all the hero-worship of an adolescent.

'Is he abroad now?' Andrew asked.

'No. He's working on a site in Yorkshire. I haven't seen too much of him while he was up there, just the occasional weekend visit home.'

'That's Suffolk, isn't it?' Andrew had heard her mention once or twice that she was going home to her family in Suffolk.

She nodded, her green eyes bright.

'Town or country?' he asked as if he really wanted to know.

'A cottage in the country,' she told him. 'Near the sea at Ryham.'

'Nice country around there,' he nodded.

'Very remote,' she said, betraying that she regarded that as an advantage. 'Peaceful and isolated.'

He looked down at her, his eyes skimming over the sleek dark hair, the cool oval face, the tranquil green eyes as they visualised her home. 'It sounds like the perfect background for you,' he said, surprising her.

They arrived at her floor and she got out, smiling as the doors closed on him again. They had earlier agreed to have a rest for an hour after lunch, partly to aid digestion, partly to give each of them some time to themselves. They would meet beside the pool later.

Claire rested on her bed, her eyes closed, fighting off thoughts of Nick whenever they tried to invade her head, but the struggle was weakening, so after a while she got up and took a cool shower, grimacing at her naked reflection in the mirror afterwards. Surely she should have learnt some self-defence by now? She was wide open to him, even though her mind insisted on facing the danger he represented to her peace. Pull yourself together, she silently told herself.

She slid into her bikini, then paused, a frown on her forehead. Was it frowned on here to wear them? In some countries she knew it was, but Andrew hadn't warned her about this one. Shrugging, she found her matching beach coat and put it on. If Andrew told her she couldn't wear the bikini she could always just sit around in the beach coat for a while.

When she wandered out on to the patio surrounding the blue-watered pool, she stopped abruptly, facing Nick. He was alone there, drinking a long, cool glass of Martini and lemonade under a floral umbrella, the hard brown body leaning back in a white wicker chair, one leg crossed over the other, his bare feet wet from the pool.

He lifted his dark brows. 'Don't just stand there,' he commanded. 'Come over here.'

Claire lifted her head, summoning her spirit, and walked over to join him, while he watched her graceful, long-limbed body out of blue eyes which flickered up and down over her, taking in everything: the lime green coat which ended at her white thighs, the plunging lapels which laid bare her throat and the beginning of her breasts, her flushed face and over-bright eyes.

'Why the wrap?' he asked lazily. 'Too hot here to need it.'

'I wasn't sure whether bikinis were allowed here,' she told him.

'Sure they are,' he nodded. 'So long as you wear them around the hotel pool and not wandering around the beach—down there, the best thing that could happen to you would be getting arrested. The worst would be that before the police got to you, you'd be fighting off an army of excited Arabs.'

She sat down hesitantly. 'I won't wear it around the beach,' she said lightly. She turned her head to cover the nervousness she was feeling about being so close to him, and stared at the pool. 'It looks very inviting.' The sun glinted on the bright blue water as if it beckoned her. Standing up, she unbelted her beach coat and slid out of it, laying it over her chair. Nick whistled under his breath and she blushed.

'Have a drink first,' he invited quickly, beckoning the waiter.

'Later,' she said, eyes averted.

He reached out a long brown hand and caught her wrist as she moved away. 'Now,' he said quietly, his voice insistent.

She hesitated, wondering whether to try to pull her hand free under the waiter's inquisitive stare or to submit docilely, then compromised by sitting down again, her face very pink, saying crossly, 'Have it your own way, then.'

'I intend to,' he said, and he was not just referring to the drink, his blue eyes narrowed to make that clear to her.

He ordered her drink, smiling at the waiter, who

grinned back at him, his eyes approving Nick's victory over her.

She was irritated by this male conspiracy, the silent backslapping which passed in their exchanged look. When the waiter had gone, she burst out furiously, 'Stop ordering me around, Nick!'

He didn't answer. He was too busy inspecting the slender, curved body at his leisure, his blue eyes wandering over her as if she were an object for sale in a shop window. 'I like you in green,' he said in those lazy tones. 'I like you in bikinis.'

She ignored him, so he hitched his chair nearer, catching her off guard. The long brown hand moved silkily over her naked thigh and she sat up straight, just as the waiter approached with her drink. Nick didn't remove his hand from her. The strong fingers crept over her skin, stroking it, and she glared at him, pushing his hand away. The waiter, wearing a big grin, put down her glass and moved off again, staring at them over his shoulder.

'You did that deliberately,' she accused him.

He grinned at her. 'It amused both of us,' he admitted shamelessly. 'I enjoyed it and so did he. They understand how to treat women out here. None of this equality nonsense—women are as much propety as goats or camels.' His eyes mocked her. 'Your boss would approve of that—he takes the same view, doesn't he?' The smile died out of the blue glance and menace crept into it. 'So it's time he got it straight about whose property you are, Claire, and I'm going to make sure he knows today. I'm not sitting around watching him paw my wife under my nose.'

She was panic-stricken. She did not want Andrew to

know about her marriage. He would ask too many questions and she did not want to have to give any answers. 'Don't, Nick,' she muttered, pleading with him.

He studied her expressionlessly, leaning back, his hand dangling beside the chair. 'What do I get in exchange?' he asked softly.

She felt heat sweep up her throat at the look in the blue eyes. 'What do you mean?' she croaked, her voice hoarse, as though the blush covering it was making it dry.

'As I said,' he drawled, 'I'm not sitting around any longer just watching him touch you the way he does. If there's going to be any touching done, I'm going to do it.'

She stared at him, trembling.

'You're an expert on giving men the hands-off treatment,' he added coolly. 'So give it to Knight and start now.'

The unspoken rider echoed in his voice. If not . . .

'Andrew would wonder what on earth was going on,' she said quickly, her eyes shifting under his gaze.

'Too bad,' he snapped. 'I've been wondering that myself. You've worked for him for a year. Is what I've seen just the tip of the iceberg, or is that how far he's got with you, just putting his arm round you and leering at you from time to time?'

'He does not leer!'

'That's what it looks like to me,' he said sourly.

'Your eyesight was never very keen,' she told him coldly.

He ran his eyes over the lime green bikini and what it did not cover. 'I wouldn't say that,' he drawled, grinning as the colour flushed into her features again.

Claire drank quickly, her eyes on her glass, trying to make up her mind which presented the worst problem —letting Nick tell Andrew that they were married, or having to give Andrew the cold shoulder after having encouraged him all day to think she was interested in him. She sighed. There was really no choice. Telling Andrew the truth now would be too embarrassing and painful. She was certain he would sack her. She'd lied to him for a year, and ever since they got to the hotel she had been hiding the fact that she was Nick's wife. Andrew would be bound to be suspicious, angry and very curious.

'Made up your mind?' Nick asked.

She gave him a bitter look. 'Yes. What choice do I have?'

He grinned. 'None,' he agreed cheerfully, then stood up and pulled her out of her chair. 'Let's swim,' he said, tugging at her hand.

Claire dived into the pool and surfaced in the blue water to find him doing a graceful crawl a few feet away. She began to swim herself, but felt her ankles suddenly seized by powerful hands which dragged her, struggling and squawking, down into the water. Her hair was wrenched from its combs by one of his hands, while he held her captive; then, with the long black hair floating around her face, he wrapped both arms round her body holding her hard against him, his mouth finding hers.

Claire was too shaken off balance to resist. The hard, warm pressure of his mouth deepened as he felt her helpless response. Her arms slid round his neck and laughter curved her lips as she felt the upward drag which was sending his own hair floating through her fingers as if it were a bed of seaweed.

She was still in his arms, her mouth open under his, as he kicked vigorously, sending them both shooting back to the surface before they were out of oxygen.

As their entwined bodies hit the blue surface her deafened ears dimly caught the abrupt sound of amused, delighted applause, clapping and laughing. She opened her sun-dazzled eyes to stare upwards and saw the TV team gathered around the pool in their swimming clothes, grinning down at them in astonished amusement. A little to one side stood Andrew his body clenched in anger.

Nick made no effort to release her. His face mocking, he bowed his head to his friends. 'Glad we amused you,' he said lightly. 'I found a mermaid in the pool, so I'm giving her the kiss of life.'

'Why don't I find things like that?' Wazi wailed. 'All I ever find at the seaside are Coke bottles and candy bar wrappers!'

'You haven't got the right technique,' Nick told him.

'We can see you have,' Philippa said, and Claire felt a breath of deep relief at the real amusement in the other girl's eyes. She had been afraid Philippa liked Nick, but there was no jealousy in those leonine eyes now, only clear glinting amusement and a peculiar brightness, as though Philippa was pleased to see her in Nick's arms.

Claire put her hands on Nick's wet shoulders, pushing at him, but he turned his head to shake his hair out of his eyes and grin. 'No, you don't, my girl,' he said too softly for anyone to hear. 'In my arms you are and in my arms you'll stay, while your boss takes it in.'

'He's already had time to take it in,' she said as quietly, her green eyes angry.

'I intend to make it very plain that he's not in the running,' Nick muttered, tightening his hold on her. 'Is he, Claire?' And the question was uttered tersely.

She didn't have time to answer before the team began diving into the pool, splashing them as they hit the water around them. Nick looked up at Andrew, still standing grimly on the stones around the pool, his gaze fixed on them.

The bright blue eyes glittered like the sunlit water around them. Nick turned his head and looked into her eyes. 'Kiss me,' he said, the words arrogantly imperative.

'Nick!' Her voice pleaded.

He stared into her eyes, running his long hands over her back. She trembled in sudden hunger and leant forward to put her mouth on his.

Nick gave a groan and pulled her closer, kissing her back hungrily. Claire had denied herself the sweetness of surrendering to him for so long that now she was almost frantic, snatching this moment from time's thieving grip because there might be no other chance to yield herself to her own starving need of him.

When he slowly drew back, she could sense that he had totally forgotten Andrew and the reason why he had forced her to make this public declaration. His eyes were flaring smokily on her face and his features were taut with passion.

'Come up to my room,' he whispered thickly.

'No, Nick,' she said with the last fine thread of her control on the point of snapping, knowing that if he pressed her now she would go with him, whatever the nightmares she would suffer afterwards.

'Damn you,' he said bitterly, releasing her, then shot

away, his lean body cutting through the blue waters at great speed.

Andrew walked to the side of the pool and leaned forward, extending his hand. She looked up at him, shaking back her wet black hair, then allowed him to pull her out of the water. He turned and walked to the table, sitting down, and she joined him.

'What did he use? A blowtorch?' Andrew asked bitterly, staring at her.

She picked up her glass and drank what was left in it, summoning all her spirit. 'He's very attractive,' she shrugged, not quite meeting his eyes.

'So it seems.' Andrew snapped at the waiter and ordered two drinks. Claire flicked a look into the pool and saw Nick's dark head bobbing in the water beside Philippa. He turned his face towards her, his eyes on her, and the message in them was clear enough.

Leaving Philippa, he swam over to the side and drawled, 'Come back here, Claire.'

She felt hot colour rising in her face at the insolent demand of the voice. For a few seconds she was tempted to dare him to do as he threatened, then she lost her nerve and got up. She heard Andrew make a furious sound behind her, but she walked to the side of the pool and looked down at Nick, her eyes rebellious. He lifted a hand to her ankle, stroking her calf.

'I want you with me,' he said loudly.

'You bastard,' she whispered with shaking lips.

He laughed and his hand jerked her off balance into the water. She was back in his arms as she struggled to surface, and he laughed into her face, his eyes very bright.

'Little coward,' he whispered, but now there was

warm amusement in his voice and she felt herself melting under the smile in the blue eyes. 'Come and play,' he invited. 'You haven't forgotten how to play, have you, darling?'

From somewhere the team had found a ball and were tossing it from one to the other with laughing shouts. They formed a circle and Nick pushed Claire into the middle. The ball flew about over her head while she vainly leapt to reach it and Nick laughed at her, then Wazi deliberately pitched his throw low enough for her to catch it triumphantly.

'Just as I suspected,' Nick taunted him with a grin. 'You've got a soft spot for green eyes.'

'It's what goes with them that I fancy,' Wazi said solemnly, his eyes mischievous.

'Tough,' shrugged Nick, not entirely joking. 'I never share. What's mine is mine.'

There was an odd, brief silence after this remark and Claire felt herself flush deeply under the sudden quick stares she got from them all. Nick had meant it to impress; he had said it deliberately. He was staking his claim openly, and it was the first time he had ever done so except when he married her. Now all his friends were there as witnesses, and she felt trapped.

Philippa swam towards the side of the pool and climbed out, joining Andrew at the table. Claire looked after her, wondering if she was jealous after all, and thought suddenly, too bad, he's mine, which made her feel oddly elated and alarmed at the same time, because for so long she had refused to think in terms of possession.

After she left Nick she had faced the fact that she had to give up all claim to him. He had been free to do as he liked during the past year. She wondered if there had been other women. There had been girls before her, she knew that; he had been frank about it. There had been no details, no names or memories, but he had said bluntly, 'I'm not fond of celibacy, Claire. I never have been. I've never knowingly hurt anyone before, though. All my relationships have been lighthearted and generally rather brief.' At the time she had thought romantically that the brevity had been caused by knowing that he had not found the right lover, but now she guessed that his job had ended a lot of his romances, as it had theirs. The others might not have minded the way she did, but he had always been flying away, leaving them before any roots could be put down.

Her heart missed a beat. They had begun to put down roots that first day. Those long, serious exchanges of details about each other had done just that. Had Nick done that deliberately? Or had his searching questions been fuelled simply by a driving desire to know her as intimately as he possibly could? She had felt like that about him.

Nick looked at her suddenly, his eyes probing her face. 'Feel like another drink?' he asked casually.

He pulled her out of the water and they wandered over to the table. Andrew was silent, holding his glass. Philippa was eyeing him with a sober expression. Claire sat down beside Nick and he threw an arm around her back, leaning towards her intimately. 'You're going to look like a boiled lobster tomorrow morning,' he said. 'You'd better not stay out here for much longer—that sun can be lethal.'

'You're right,' she said, seizing on the opportunity to escape. 'I think I'll go in now.'

Nick leaned over and picked up her beach coat, flinging it round her shoulders. 'Come on, then,' he said, making her heart sink. It hadn't occurred to her that he would openly accompany her. She hesitated, but his hand was under her elbow, propelling her away from the others, who grinned after them as they walked away. Only Andrew sat silent, his attitude unbending.

Once in the elevator and alone with him, Claire turned on Nick angrily. 'I hope you're satisfied now!'

His look was amused, mocking. 'Not yet,' he drawled.

She flushed deeper at that. 'Stop it, Nick!'

He looked her up and down, a brow quizzically lifted. 'A year is a long, long time to go hungry, honey.'

It was, she thought in sudden yearning. It was, indeed, and she had to be out of her mind to think of refusing him when every cell in her body was clamouring for him. She bit her lower lip, worrying it between her teeth, her eyes on the floor, and felt him watching her wryly.

'I'm not asking for anything you don't want to give me,' he said coolly.

'Don't,' she muttered.

'All right, so our marriage is over,' he said. 'I'll buy that. But does that mean the end of everything? We're both adults and it's perfectly legal.' The elevator stopped at her floor and she slowly moved to the door. He stayed where he was, staring at her averted face.

Claire felt as if her feet were embedded in wet cement. Every step dragged. She had to force herself to move with the last ounce of her will power.

'I want you,' he said suddenly, hoarsely, and she gave a faint, stifled gasp, beginning to shake.

Nick was out beside her in a second, his arm reaching

for her. The elevator closed behind him and he pushed her down the corridor towards her room, the afternoon sunshine glittering around them through the floor-length plate glass windows which lined one side of the corridor. Blindly she stared into the sunlight. The dark shadow of a mosque flickered against the blue sky. Nick took her key from her nerveless hand and opened the door of her room, propelling her inside it before he closed it behind both of them with a sound which made her pulses begin to race violently.

'Now,' he said huskily, leaning against it and staring at her.

CHAPTER FIVE

SHE felt something close in her throat, a sensation of
dark anguish. Turning her back on him, she walked to
the window and her hand closed helplessly over the
lowered blind which was throwing a soft shadow over
the room.

'I can't,' she muttered, wishing she knew a way to
stop the trembling which had seized her whole body.

Nick laughed brusquely but made no reply. Claire
heard him move and stiffened, waiting for him to ap-
proach her, but he walked to the bed and she heard him
begin to lie down on it, the springs creaking under his
weight.

Pulling her coat closer around her, she said, 'You're
still damp. You'll make the bed damp.'

'Too bad,' he said indifferently.

She turned then and looked across the room at him.
He was lying full length, his arms crossed under the
dark head, watching her without a smile, and the look
in the blue eyes made her heart thud.

'Can't we talk?' she asked desperately. 'We're not
animals.'

'If I'm behaving like one, it's what you've reduced
me to,' he threw back baldly.

'That's not fair!'

'Grow up,' he snapped. 'You refuse to think or be-
have like an adult. When we took those marriage vows
I seem to remember something about for better, for

worse . . . don't you ever mean a word of what you promise? Only a few weeks later you walked out on me.'

'Can't you try to understand how I feel? I'm terrified, Nick. You may be used to risking your life day after day, but I'm not going to sit in England waiting for some official to tell me you're dead.'

'So rather than risk getting hurt you refuse to live at all,' he said contemptuously. 'Great! What a little heroine!'

'I never pretended to be a heroine!'

'You're not even a woman,' he said scathingly.

Whiteness flowed up her face and she bent her head, her damp black hair falling around her oval features. He watched her, his mouth tight.

'Please go,' she said huskily.

'I'm damned if I will.'

'You promised to divorce me.'

'Maybe I will,' he said coolly. 'But right now divorce isn't what's on my mind, and I'm pretty sure it isn't on yours, either.'

She looked at him miserably, her mouth quivering. 'Please, Nick . . . not like this. It makes it so brutal.'

'You've made it pretty clear you don't want it any other way,' he said, his face hard. 'When we got married I gave you all the gentleness I'm capable of and you threw it back into my face. From now on, we'll deal together on the level it seems you understand best, so stop playing hard to get and come over here.'

'No,' she said, lifting her head in a bitter gesture.

'If I have to come and get you, I'll make you sorry,' he promised silkily.

'Then that's the way it's going to be,' she said wildly. 'I'm not going to make it easy for you. You'll have to use force, and I can promise you, you won't enjoy it much.'

His eyes darkened with anger. He came off the bed with the spring of a leopard and was beside her before she had time to draw breath, his hands violent as he lifted her off her feet and into his arms. She fought in cold desperation, hating him. Her brain kept presenting her with memories of their brief time together, the love and laughter they had once shared, until it all dissolved into misery and fear, and the cool determination he was showing now was intolerable. Once they had gone into each other's arms naturally, eagerly. Now she could only feel the dark pressure of his desire for her with nothing behind it which spoke of the old love.

Nick threw her on to the bed and his weight held her down, his hands thrust into her loose, flowing black hair. There was contempt in the blue eyes as they ran over her white face.

'Now we'll see who's going to enjoy what,' he said grimly.

Claire twisted to evade the searching mouth. His hands jerked her head round, controlling her by pain, his fingers pulling at her long hair.

'Don't,' she muttered before the hard mouth silenced her. She tried desperately to stop the reaction which flowed up inside her, but his lips forcibly parted hers and the pent-up hunger erupted in her body. 'Nick,' she groaned under his mouth, her hands pressing up his bare chest to the wide, strong shoulders, hearing his heart beat close to her, his skin warm and filled with life under her fingers.

She felt her own senses spring into furious life. He only had to touch her, she thought miserably, for everything else to cease to matter and only what was happening between them to have any validity. Behind her closed eyelids a white radiance burnt on her retina, dazzling her. Her hands clung to the hard, brown throat, pulling his head down to retain the heat of his mouth on her.

She was so totally absorbed by him that the hard rapping on the door passed unnoticed for a moment, except that she vaguely thought at first that it was the sound of her own heart beating. Then she came out of her daze to realise that someone was demanding her by name, and Nick lifted his head, frowning darkly.

'Who the hell——?' He sounded as dazed as she felt, his voice thickened by passion.

'Claire!' It was Andrew's voice, she realised with a start, and she looked at Nick, her face burning. 'I want to get some work done,' Andrew called, banging again. 'There are some phone calls to be made.'

'Damn him!' Nick muttered, his dark brows jerking together.

'I have to open the door,' she said nervously.

'Ignore him!'

'I can't. He's my boss.' She pushed at the heavy body, her face flushed. 'Please, Nick.'

He rolled away, swearing under his breath. Claire jumped off the bed and watched as he walked to the door and opened it. Andrew stared at him, his eyes narrowed, an angry expression in his face. Nick gave him an insolent look in reply, turned his dark head to eye Claire coldly and said lightly, 'Be seeing you, honey,' before sauntering lazily away.

Andrew looked after him, looked back at Claire, his brown eyes shifting icily from her flushed, dishevelled appearance to the rumpled bed. His brow was level with distaste

'Get dressed,' he said. 'I'll see you in my room in ten minutes—and be on time.'

When he had gone she covered her face with her hands and shook with misery. It took her a few moments to recover her ability to control her feelings. When she was able to move without feeling as though an iron spike were being forced through her head, she hurriedly changed into her white dress and brushed her hair, deftly pinning it back into its usual chignon. She applied make-up quickly, surveyed herself unsmilingly in the mirror and left her room, her head held high.

Andrew let her into his room and walked away without a word, his hands thrust into his pockets. She stood there, her hands clenched at her sides, feeling sick.

He turned on his heel, leaning against the window, and stared at her fixedly.

'Well? Do I get an explanation? Or do I take it that you were swept off your feet by our Don Juan of a television personality?'

Quietly, she said, 'I'm your secretary, Andrew, nothing more, and my private life is my own affair. I thought we'd agreed on that.'

His mouth thinned. 'Not when you make it so public,' he snapped. 'You let him make a fool of me out there!'

Her eyes widened in surprise. 'A fool of you?'

'Don't pretend to be dumb,' he said bitterly. 'What do you think they all thought when you let him walk off with you like that?'

She was baffled. 'What has it got to do with you what I do? You're my boss, not my boy-friend.'

His jaw clenched. 'It never occurred to you that they thought there was anything between us?'

She flushed. 'What they thought makes no difference. We both know that there's nothing between us, there never has been.'

Dark red colour swept up to his hairline. 'You know perfectly well that since we got here you've been acting as though there was,' he said unanswerably.

She looked away. 'I'm sorry if I gave the wrong impression.'

'Don't sound so innocent,' he told her sharply. 'You allowed them to believe you were more than just my secretary, then you publicly dumped me for Waring. If you were that desperate for a man, you should have made your signals a bit stronger.'

Her eyes flashed. 'That's insulting! I wasn't giving any signals.'

'Like hell you weren't! I thought I was finally getting somewhere with you all morning, then I come out to the pool and find you behaving like . . .'

'Don't say it,' she broke in furiously. 'You've got no right to say such things to me.'

'What do you expect? Ever since you came to work for me, you've behaved like an ice maiden, but Waring is only on the scene for two days and he has you practically begging.' His brown eyes were flaming. 'What has that bastard got? He has that blonde eating out of his hand, yet he walks off with you openly and she doesn't even blink.'

'There's nothing between Nick and Philippa,' she burst out, her voice ragged.

Andrew sneered. 'Don't be a little fool. They're lovers—it sticks out a mile.'

'If they were, do you really think she would let him go off with me without a protest?' she asked.

He shrugged. 'They play very funny games in that world. Maybe they both experiment from time to time. Who cares? If that's the sort of life she fancies let her enjoy it, but it isn't your sort of world, is it, Claire? No decent girl would stand for it.'

She felt tired, depressed. 'I'm sorry if you felt humiliated by the way I behaved this afternoon,' she said in low tones. 'But I've never given you any reason to suppose you had any rights over me.'

He made an impatient sound, staring at her. 'I'm disappointed in you, Claire. I never expected to see you fall flat on your face for a chap like that.'

She laughed wildly.

'What's funny?' Andrew demanded roughly. 'That's how it looked to me, to everyone who watched you with him. He's an insolent swine and you let him do just as he liked with you.'

'Not quite,' she said wryly.

Andrew stared at her. There was a silence and she met his eyes levelly.

'When he was in your room——' Andrew began thickly.

'Please!' She turned away, her oval face deeply flushed. 'I think we should curtail this discussion. I thought you wanted to get some work done.'

'That was just an excuse and you know it,' he retorted. 'I wanted to stop him before it went too far.'

Claire turned on him angrily. 'You had no right to interfere!'

'I'm sorry if I spoilt your fun,' he said tightly. 'Never mind, I'm sure he'll make it with you tonight.' He smiled unpleasantly. 'If he isn't too busy with his blonde girl-friend.'

The biting tone of his voice stung for a second, but she was suddenly curious. Although he seemed angry about the way she had behaved with Nick she got the feeling that Philippa's involvement irked him a lot more.

She stared at him closely. 'I think you fancy her,' she said abruptly.

The flush which ran up his face was dark with anger. 'You what? Are you kidding? The only thing I'd like to do to her is slap her silly.'

'And then what?' Claire asked drily, her eyes on his face.

'Then nothing,' Andrew bit out. 'Don't try to foist that female on to me, because I wouldn't touch her with a bargepole. Everything about her infuriates me. Why Waring looks twice at her I'll never know, but don't tell me she isn't his mistress, because I wouldn't believe you. I've seen them dancing together and even in those revolting jeans she wears it's obvious.'

Claire lowered her lashes and watched him through them. 'I wonder what she's like in bed . . .'

Andrew drew a harsh breath. 'I can imagine,' he said tersely. 'It would be like going to bed with a wildcat.'

'Have you been imagining it, Andrew?' she asked softly.

His face closed up. 'If you're trying to distract me from the subject of Waring, forget it,' he told her. 'I'll admit that I have no jurisdiction over your private life, but while we're out here we are representing the firm, and I won't have you tarnishing the firm's name with escapades like this one.'

Claire was in an impossible position. If she refused to let Nick have his own way, he would inform Andrew of their marriage, and Andrew would shower her with angry questions about it. If she saw much more of Nick, Andrew would be furious with her. Either way she was in trouble. She sighed deeply, her face troubled.

'Do you hear me, Claire?' he demanded.

'Of course I hear you,' she said wearily.

'I mean what I say.'

'I realise you do,' she said. The writing was on the wall. Sooner or later she was going to have to resign. Whatever she did now, Andrew was going to be annoyed with her. Running into Nick again had destroyed the quiet sanctuary which had been her job with Andrew during this past year. In a way, that was the least of her problems; Nick had forced her to admit that to herself. Other things were pressing on her mind, and her job was suddenly the least painful of the issues confronting her.

Andrew made a rough sound under his breath and she looked at him, her green eyes wide.

'Get me London on the phone,' he said flatly.

Quietly she obeyed and stood, listening, while he spoke curtly to head office about some mix-up over bookings made in England. 'Send a rocket to the people responsible,' he snapped. 'We don't want to get a name for that sort of muddle.'

She could imagine the wry look on the face of the person at the end of that blistering comment. Andrew, in this mood, was as charming as an iron bar. Claire sensed that he was taking out his frustrated inability to act about Nick on the unfortunate at the other end of the line. It was typical of him. He was not a man who liked to feel impotent. He enjoyed the power his position gave him, and he did not take kindly to frustration of any kind.

Although he had behaved like a jealous man over Nick, she was somehow convinced that he was not interested in her in any real sense. Although he had made a few light passes in her direction since they were in Keravi she had never felt that he meant any of them seriously, and his present mood puzzled her.

He put the phone down and glanced at her with a stiff expression. 'You'd better remember what I said, Claire,' he told her. 'They're all dining with us tonight, remember. Steer clear of Waring. I won't put up with being made to look a fool twice in one day. You're with me tonight, whether as my secretary or not.'

She stared down at her feet. 'Am I to dress for dinner?'

'Certainly you are,' he said. 'I want you to look your best. At the least, you can show that blonde termagant how to look like a woman.'

Claire shot him a curious look. 'Pull out all the stops, you mean?' Her eyes narrowed. 'Am I going as your trophy or your shield, Andrew?'

He reddened. 'What the hell is that supposed to mean?'

'Do you want her to be jealous or scared off?' she asked softly.

'Neither,' he said curtly. 'I just want her to get a lesson in how to make a man look twice.'

'Right,' she said casually, moving to the door. 'Although I doubt if she needs one. She may not wear Paris fashions, but she's very bright and very attractive.'

'Like hell she is,' he snapped, turning his back.

Claire went down to her own room and spent a long time getting ready, a peculiar excitement throbbing in her veins. She had already forgotten Andrew. She dressed for Nick, her hands shaking, and when she was ready she went down in the elevator with a sense of unbearable anticipation.

Andrew was already in the bar with most of the TV team. Their heads swung to stare as she walked towards them, her long-limbed body floating gracefully in the cornflower-printed dress. Wazi whistled softly, his eyes bright. Andrew stood up and the others followed, smiling at her. She let her smile drift over them briefly and sat down.

Andrew summoned the barman and ordered her drink. 'You look very charming,' he told her with approval.

'Why don't our secretaries look like that?' Wazi asked in plaintive tones.

Claire sipped her drink, disappointed to find that Nick had not yet arrived. Neither, she saw, had Philippa. Wazi talked casually about Keravi, shaking his head over the changes which were going to follow in the wake of progress. 'The cultural shock hasn't begun to hit them yet,' he said. 'When it does . . . wham! Centuries of custom will fly out of the window and they won't know what's hit them.'

'Progress has to be paid for,' Andrew said dogmatically. 'They need the money for hospitals, schools, roads . . .'

'Maybe,' Wazi agreed. 'But it's coming too fast and they'll be swamped by it.' He gave Andrew a patient look. 'Remember, Europe took years to reach the level of progress we're foisting on to Keravi. You want it all to happen at once over here. The people aren't prepared for it . . .' He broke off, his eyes swivelling to the door and made a little sound of astonishment and amusement. 'Well, well, well,' he drawled.

Andrew casually turned his head then froze. Claire looked round and saw Philippa in a metallic black dress which glittered as she walked, the silken material clinging seductively to her curved body. Her blonde hair had been set in a cluster of curls around her head, giving her the alluring look of a handsome boy. Around her brown throat glinted the heavy barbaric silver of an Arabic necklace.

'You look fantastic,' Claire said frankly, smiling at her.

'The transformation scene,' Wazi commented, grinning, his black eyes sweeping down over her. 'Just as well you don't come to work looking like that or we wouldn't get any done!'

Andrew sat staring into his drink as Philippa sat down facing him. There was a stiff look about his shoulders and neck as Wazi ordered Philippa a drink.

'We're going to have quite an evening,' Philippa murmured to Claire. Her eyes glinted with amusement. 'Six of them to two of us—that makes three each. Do we spin a coin, or just pick our own team?'

Claire laughed. 'Take it as it comes, I think.'

'And it will certainly come,' Wazi assured her wickedly. 'With you two looking the way you do, we'll be fighting over you by the time we get to the coffee!'

'Is that so?' drawled Nick from behind her chair.

Wazi laughed. 'Hi, Nick. Take a look at our Pippa. Isn't she a knockout?'

'Fantastic,' Nick agreed, his hands coming down on Claire's shoulders, their warmth burning through the thin material of her bolero.

Andrew lifted his head belligerently and glared at him. 'Claire is with me,' he said through his teeth. 'Stick with your own lady-friend.'

There was a taut silence. Nick showed his teeth in a brittle, barbed smile. 'Watch yourself, my friend. I've been aching to knock your teeth down your throat since I set eyes on you. Much more of it and I will!'

Andrew pushed back his chair and stood up, squaring his shoulders. 'Try it,' he offered through his teeth.

'Delighted,' said Nick, tense as a coiled spring, but Claire jumped up and caught his arm as he swung for Andrew's jaw.

'Don't, please!'

'No, don't!' Philippa said sharply. 'Remember where you are, for God's sake, Nick. We don't want to find ourselves shoved into an Arab jail.'

'Then tell your womanising boy-friend to leave my secretary alone,' Andrew snapped, turning his head, his brown eyes flaming at her.

'I'll tell you,' Nick said tersely. 'I'll do as I please with my wife!'

Andrew's head swung sharply. There was a silence in which you could have heard a pin drop. Slowly, Andrew looked down at Claire. She was pale, her eyes stretched wide in shock.

'What's he talking about?' he demanded.

She bit her lower lip, not knowing how to reply.

'Tell him, Claire,' Nick commanded in curt tones.

She sat down. 'You tell him,' she threw back. 'You've started it—you carry on.'

Philippa was staring at her, blank incredulity on her face. The rest of the team were staring down at their glasses, keeping all expression off their faces.

Claire picked up her own drink and sipped it, ignoring them all, feeling suddenly like throwing the glass at Nick's sardonic face.

'Well, Waring?' Andrew asked. 'What did you mean, your wife? Claire has never been married.'

'Like hell she hasn't,' Nick retorted, his voice burning with temper. 'We've been married for more than a year.'

'I don't believe you,' said Andrew, his voice stiff with shock. 'Why should she hide the fact? When we arrived and met you, she never said a word to me. You met like total strangers.'

'Some marriages are like that,' Nick said cynically. 'Her reasons for keeping quiet are none of your business.'

'As her employer I have a right to know,' Andrew told him.

'She just resigned,' said Nick.

Claire felt her spine tighten with rage, but she did not look round. She had known she was going to resign ever since the afternoon, but she was infuriated with Nick for making such a declaration. He had no right to say it.

'I didn't hear her,' Andrew snapped.

'You heard me.'

'Even if you are her husband, which I doubt, it doesn't give you any right to make her decisions for her!' Andrew said tightly.

'I'll decide what rights I have,' Nick said blandly.

Andrew looked down at Claire's black head. 'Haven't you got anything to say, Claire?'

'You heard her,' Nick broke in. 'She told me to do

the talking, and I'm doing it.'

'Claire . . .' Andrew began thickly.

'Sit down, both of you,' Philippa told them icily. 'You're behaving like schoolboys!' She looked across the table at Claire's white face. 'Are you a Londoner, Claire?' Her voice held a polite interest.

'No, I come from Suffolk,' Claire told her. 'What about you?'

'Oh, I'm a Londoner,' Philippa said. 'Shall we have another drink? I think we all need one.' She waved a hand at the fascinated barman, who came hurriedly over with black eyes which burned with curiosity. 'Same again all round,' Philippa said calmly. When he had gone, she smiled at Claire. 'Do your family still live in Suffolk?'

Andrew slowly sank into his seat and Nick moved off to get another chair which he deliberately slid in between Claire and Andrew, seating himself, his arm around Claire's shoulders. She ignored him, her chin raised defiantly. The waiter brought the drinks and they all gratefully sipped at them.

Tactfully, Wazi began to talk about his children, and Philippa encouraged him with light questions. The rest of the team joined in, teasing Wazi unmercifully about some snapshots he produced from a jacket pocket. They were passed round the table from hand to hand, pictures of a slim dark girl with smiling eyes and two babies, set against a background of English countryside which was peculiarly nostalgic to Claire in this alien background.

Nick coolly joined in with the teasing, shaking his head over the pictures. 'Poor kids, they even look like you,' he told Wazi, who grinned, delighted.

Andrew put down his glass and stood up. 'Shall we eat?' he asked coldly.

They all trooped after him into the dining-room. Andrew sat down at the large table, his eyes fixed on the cloth, and they took their seats in an awkward silence. The waiters hovered eagerly to take their order, and they all made a pretence of deep interest in the menu. Claire sat at Andrew's right with Nick beside her. He leaned his elbow on the table, his head inclined towards her ear and whispered, 'Stop sulking.'

'You're a bastard!' she hissed back.

'That's right,' he agreed coolly. 'I'm your husband, though. You can't deny that.'

'Not for long.'

'For as long as I want you,' he said, his mouth against her ear, sending a shiver along her spine.

'How long is that?' she asked involuntarily.

He laughed softly, and she moved away from him, annoyed with herself for having asked.

Under cover of his own menu, Andrew was staring at them. Claire felt the anger in his eyes and looked down at the printed words, but they swam in front of her meaninglessly.

She looked up across the table and met Philippa's intent gaze. A flush grew on her cheeks and she looked away again. She had blithely told Andrew that there was nothing between Philippa and Nick, but why was she so sure? She of all people knew how irresistible he could be when he chose, and her heart quickened jealously.

They all ordered and a brittle conversation broke out around the table. Andrew took no part in it, his attitude grim. Philippa leaned back against her chair, laughing at some remark by Wazi, and her napkin slid to the floor. She bent to pick it up just as Andrew bent down for the same purpose and their heads collided. Andrew swore under his breath and straightened. Philippa picked up her napkin and sat up again, her mouth wry.

'I'm sorry,' she said to him.

'That's all right,' he muttered. 'I've got used to getting my head thumped every time I see you.'

Claire felt Nick stiffen beside her and slid her hand over his thigh. He looked at her, then placed his own hand over hers, pressing it against him. Blushing, she slid it away.

They ate in the same difficult atmosphere, but gradually the bottles of champagne thawed the ice, even that which encased Andrew. His manner eased. His skin grew flushed. He drank more than usual, his eyes on Philippa's averted face.

None of them seemed disposed, however, to linger over the coffee. As soon as they had finished it the majority of the team made polite excuses and left, thanking Andrew for his hospitality in a guarded way. Nick and Claire were left at the table with Andrew and Philippa, and the atmosphere between the four of them was tense.

'Let's go and dance,' said Nick, rising, pulling Claire after him, his hand around her wrist.

She did not want to struggle with him in public, so she went, her face tense. When they were outside in the foyer, she turned on him angrily.

'You had no business to tell Andrew like that! You ruined the evening for everybody and made a scene in front of the other guests.'

'I warned you,' he said flatly. 'No one tells me to leave my own wife alone.'

'What gave you the right to tell him I resigned?' she asked, shifting her ground

'This,' he said, his hands hard on her shoulders, his mouth hot on her own.

She pulled away from him, breathing fast. They stared at each other in silence.

'Now do we take up where we left off this afternoon?' Nick asked her unsteadily.

'I want to dance,' she said, walking away.

He followed her moodily, his hands in his pockets, his eyes on the slender, graceful figure just in front of him.

He took her into his arms and they moved around the floor, their bodies close, their movements harmonious. Claire felt weary suddenly, leaning her forehead on his wide shoulder, and he pulled her closer still, his hand moving over her back.

She was aware of his face against the black silk of her hair, his breathing warm against her skin. He was all the happiness she needed, all the safety, and she wanted nothing more than to lean on him like this for ever and feel the beating of his heart above her own.

The music ended and they walked in silence back to the table at which Andrew now sat with Philippa. Drinks stood in front of them, but they were not talking.

Nick gave Philippa a quick grin. 'Thanks for ordering us a drink,' he said sarcastically.

'I wasn't sure you wanted company,' she retorted, her eyes flicking to Claire. 'You looked as if you were in another world.'

Nick laughed, giving Claire a long glance. 'We were,' he said.

She blushed, but her eyes were fever-bright. He called the waiter and ordered drinks, but before they came the music started again. He looked at Andrew, who was brooding over his glass, shrugged, and said to Philippa, 'Want to dance, Pippa?'

Andrew's head came up. 'You want both of them, do you?' he asked bitterly. 'Too bad. She can put up with dancing with me.' Standing up, he jerked Philippa upwards and pulled her on to the floor and into his arms. They moved away stiffly, their faces averted from each other.

Nick stared after them, then looked at Claire intently. 'He's got it badly, hasn't he?' he asked, his voice hard. 'How far had it gone, Claire? Exactly what rights did he imagine he had?'

'None,' she defended herself firmly. 'Until we arrived here, he was just my boss.'

'And since you got here?'

She might have known he would pick that up. She had given him the clear impression that Andrew and she were involved, and now she would have to put it straight, but would he believe her?

'I wanted to make you think there was something between us,' she admitted. 'For protection, that was all.'

'So you had to make him think there was something, too,' he guessed coldly.

'He's never even kissed me,' she protested.

'But he wanted to?' Nick was tight-lipped now, his blue eyes scornful, and she deserved it. She had flirted mildly with Andrew to keep Nick away and now it was rebounding on her own head.

She picked up her own drink and swallowed it, while he watched her, his brows lifting.

'Needed that, did you?' he asked sardonically.

'If you're going to be difficult, yes,' she said, her eyes brighter than ever now, her face more flushed.

'I could be bloody impossible,' he promised, leaning towards her menacingly.

'You usually are.'

He grinned suddenly. 'Do you still want to dance, or are you coming to bed yet?'

She stood up, her head whirling slightly. 'Let's dance.'

He took her in his arms, his mouth sardonic. 'Safer, is it, Claire?'

'Much,' she agreed, leaning her weight on him, her hand sliding along his shoulder towards his neck.

He held her tightly. 'Want me badly, Claire?' he asked into her ear.

'Very badly,' she muttered, her fingers stroking his hard neck.

He laughed softly. 'There's only one way to stop that,' he murmured, his mouth brushing her neck.

'Don't talk,' she said huskily. 'Dance.'

'That isn't what either of us want to do, though, is it?' he said with amusement.

She turned her head and stared at the hard, sensual mouth. 'Shut up!' she half wailed.

'Fight it as long as you can, darling,' he taunted. 'We both know where we're going to end up tonight.'

CHAPTER SIX

WHEN they drifted back to the table Claire was in a lethargic state of total weakness, her hand threaded through his arm, holding on to him in case she felt her knees giving way under her. Her skin was glowing with colour. Her eyes were bright with dreams.

Philippa looked at her as she sat down, lifting her brows. 'You look pretty high,' she teased. 'Is it Nick or the champagne?'

'Both,' Nick murmured drily.

Andrew's mouth turned down at the edges. 'Another drink?' he asked flatly, looking round for the waiter.

'No, thanks,' Nick said coolly. 'I think Claire's had enough. It's time we turned in now, anyway. She's half asleep on her feet already, and I want her wide awake right now.'

Philippa gave a rueful smile. 'Spare my blushes!'

His hands flat on the table, his jaw thrust out, Andrew threw her an icy look. 'What does he do? Mesmerise? Don't you give a damn who he takes to bed, or do you think he'll come back to you if you wait long enough?'

Nick sat up straight. 'Hey, that's enough of that! You may be feeling sick because Claire belongs to me, not you, but that's no reason for taking your malice out on Pip.'

'Pip!' Andrew spat the name out distastefully. 'You make her sound like a cartoon character, and that's just what she is . . . slouching around in filthy jeans like a street arab!'

Nick's shoulders went rigid. He began to rise, but Philippa cut in briskly, her eyes flaring. 'Ignore him, Nick. He's been getting at me all evening because he's got some fixation about you and me, God knows why.' She turned her head towards Andrew, her chin tilted. 'For the last time, Mr Knight, I'm not romantically interested in Nick, and I never have been. As far as I'm concerned, Claire's welcome to him. He doesn't turn me on. Got it?' Her voice was sarcastic, her eyes challenging.

Andrew stared at her, his eyes running over her slim, rounded body in the glittering dress. 'Then why all the show tonight?' he asked. 'Or do you expect me to believe you dressed up like a Christmas tree for me?'

'For you?' Her colour rose. Her voice rose with it. 'God almighty, you conceited bastard! What did you expect me to wear for a dinner party? My old jeans? That's my working outfit. Tonight I wore a dress, but it certainly wasn't for your benefit, it was for mine. I knew damned well Claire would look as ravishing as ever, and I wasn't sitting here while you made your usual cracks about the way I look!'

A bright gleam came into the brown eyes. Andrew leaned towards her, his jaw pugnacious. 'So it was for me,' he said thickly.

Philippa's hand flew out and contacted his face with a crack of sound. There was a moment of silence while he stared at her, his cheek darkening with the mark of her fingers. She put her hand to her mouth in shock. Andrew moved, pulling the hand down, then kissed her brutally, his strong fingers grasping her chin, immobilising her head. Taking his mouth away, he straightened and walked out of the room, the back of his neck dark red.

Nick whistled under his breath. Philippa's face was hotly flushed, her lips shaking.

She looked from one to the other of them wildly, then got up and fled without a word. Nick watched her go, his brows quizzical.

'I had a vague suspicion about that,' Claire said dreamily. Her head felt heavy and she was sleepy. 'Andrew reacted very violently whenever he set eyes on her, and it seemed very out of character for him to be quite so hostile to a woman, even though she did argue with him all the time.'

'So it wasn't you he was stalking, it was Pip,' Nick drawled, a grin curling his mouth. 'Well, good luck to him. Pip's quite a girl, but I'd say he will have his hands full if he tries to take her on. She has a brain like a knife and she's very liberated.'

Claire picked up the last word jealously. 'What exactly do you mean by that?'

He threw her a wicked look. 'Jealous, my darling?'

'Have you and Philippa ever . . .' she began, and he cut her off with an amused shake of the head.

'Alas, no,' he mourned. 'Pip said it all when she said I didn't turn her on.'

'Did you try?' Claire asked, focusing on him with difficulty.

'What do you think?' he enquired lightly, staring back at her, his mouth crooked.

'I'm asking you, damn you,' she said, beginning to yawn.

'You're out for the count, aren't you, honey?' he

asked wryly. 'My damned luck again. Come on, bed for you.'

His arm around her waist, he guided her into the elevator and they sped up to her floor. Nick helped her to her room and opened the door, then followed her into the room and deftly helped her to undress. She was too sleepy to care by now. Swaying, she stood sleepily while he slid her dress away from her, then she toppled into the bed in her brief slip, her eyes already closing. Nick bent and brushed his mouth over hers, a smile still on his face. She dreamily murmured, 'Did you, Nick?'

'Did I what, honey?' he asked.

'Fancy Philippa?' she whispered. 'A year is a long time. Were there other women?'

He laughed. 'Sleep on it and work it out for yourself,' he told her coolly. 'Goodnight, Claire.'

The light flicked off and she slid into sleep without a pause, her body lightly relaxed between the sheets, her mind already filling with deeply pleasant dreams of Nick. In her sleep the year apart had never existed and they were blissfully together, the old sunshine between them, the laughter and companionship unbroken. For months after they split up she had had nightmares about him being killed. Time after time she had got a phone call or a telegram and read it or listened, her face going deathly white, her body numb with bitter pain. Those bad dreams had haunted her for a long time. Tonight nothing of that entered her mind. They were together, as they ought to be, and she was aware of a sense of total peace.

When she woke up it was a cool blue dawn and someone was banging on the door impatiently. She frowned, lifting her head. 'Claire, for God's sake!' the voice yelled.

She slid out of bed and went over to the door, opening it with a stare of bewilderment. 'What's wrong?'

'You've got to get packed and out of here as fast as possible,' Nick said hurriedly, coming into the room fast.

'Nick, what are you talking about?' Sleep still hung on her like a cloud and her green eyes were dazed.

'Revolution,' he bit out.

Her eyes widened. The sleepy look left them. 'What?'

'There's no time to talk about it,' he snapped. 'Where are your clothes? Get dressed, for God's sake. The British Legation is pulling in all the British subjects it can reach. They plan to evacuate us today—there's a British ship just up the coast which is coming down to pick up as many as possible. You've got to get on that ship, Claire.' He was already pulling clothes out of the wardrobe and drawers, throwing them on to the bed and getting her suitcases.

'What's happening, Nick?' she asked tensely.

'Nobody knows for sure yet,' he said. 'A party of rebels have taken over the radio station and a few key points.' He flung round and made an impatient sound. 'Get dressed, girl, and move!'

She ran into the bathroom and washed her face in cold water, then went back, feeling more awake, and dressed in the olive green suit. Nick was too busy packing her clothes to notice her, but when he had finished he turned and ran a glance over her comprehensively. The blue eyes grew bright. 'You look edible,' he said drily. 'A pity I've no time to find out how good you taste.'

She found a laugh coming into her chest, but sobered. 'You're coming with me, Nick?' she asked, her voice shaking a little.

'Come on, we've got to hurry,' he answered evasively, locking her case and lifting it.

'Nick . . .' She caught at his arm, halting him in mid stride. 'Come with me, won't you? You aren't staying here?' Panic was in her tone and fear in her green eyes.

His mouth compressed. 'There's no time to argue over it now, Claire,' he said tensely. 'You know the answer to that one. So come on, get down to the foyer.'

'If you leave me now I'll never speak to you again,' she flung at his lean back. 'It will be over for good, Nick.'

He only paused so briefly that she might not have known it if she had not been nervously intent on him. He opened the door without replying and she bitterly followed him.

As they walked out into the corridor there was a strange crack of sound followed almost immediately by a noise like someone eating toffee. Nick gave a sharp cry, dropped her case, turned on his heel, seizing her hand, and pulled her back through the open door of her room, closing it after them with a bang.

Claire was too startled to realise what had happened. She stared at him, her heart thumping. 'What was that?' Then on the heels of her question she caught sight of the red stain spreading across his arm and her face went quite white. 'You're hurt!'

Nick was standing very still, his eyes narrowed, ignoring her. 'I wonder how many more there are . . .' he muttered, turning and striding to the window. Keeping his body turned sideways along the frame he lifted one of the slats in the blind and stared out. She saw his body relax. 'None that side, I think,' he said to himself.

'What's going on?' Claire asked nervously. 'Nick, your arm is bleeding! Let me look at it . . .'

'Keep away from this window!' he snapped, moving away very quickly. He went to the telephone and lifted it, jiggled with it impatiently, then made a face and slammed it down. 'Dead as a doornail . . . God!'

'What is it, Nick?' she asked again.

He sat down on the bed and stared at her. 'There's a sniper out there,' he told her crisply.

She whitened. 'A sniper? Oh, you've been shot!' She had seen nothing, only heard sounds which she did not connect.

'He's up on that damned mosque, I suspect,' said Nick. 'We can't get out through that door into the corridor, Claire. We have two choices—either we stay cooped up in here and come under mortar fire, possibly, or we try to climb along the balconies and risk coming under sniper fire from somewhere out there. If they have snipers in position on one side there may be some on the other side, although I didn't spot any.'

She came across to him without replying. 'Let me see to your arm,' she asked quietly.

'It's fine,' he said impatiently. 'Claire, are you listening?'

'You must do whatever you think best,' she said, finding a pair of scissors in her handbag and beginning to cut away his shirt very tenderly. She laid bare the wound with a wince. The blood ran freely, though, and she could see no sign of a bullet in the long wound.

'It's just a flesh wound,' he said in irritation. 'The bullet grazed along without entering anywhere.'

'Sit still,' she said. 'It must be washed. I've got some plasters in the bathroom.'

He followed her in there and impatiently stood still while she washed his arm, dried it gently and bandaged it. When she had finished he looked down at her, his mouth hard.

'We've got to get out of here, Claire. We could be caught in some nasty crossfire if we stay. You've got to get on that ship.'

She nodded. 'What about my case? You dropped it outside.'

'Damn the bloody case,' he said tautly. 'Come on, we'll try the balconies.'

She followed him across the room and he slowly slid the door open. At once there was a familiar sound and he ducked away, hurling her to the floor behind him, covering her body with his. When she looked up there was a large splintered star in the glass of the balcony door.

Nick swore. 'We're holed up here,' he said to her. For a long moment he looked into her pale face, his mouth caught between irony and concern. 'I'm afraid you're stuck here with me for a long time, my darling,' he said.

'Surely it won't be for long,' she said. 'Someone will do something.'

He laughed harshly. 'God, your sweet innocence is maddening! Don't expect the U.S. Cavalry, my darling. Only a fool would try to get us out of here now. We're pinned down on both sides. All this damned plate glass is a death-trap. The most we can hope for is a cease-fire and at this stage of the game that's pretty unlikely.'

'Oh!' she said, biting her lip.

He slowly got up. 'We're out of range here,' he said. 'Just stay away from the windows.' He turned his head to give her a sardonic glance. 'Quite without prejudice, the safest place in the room is the bed.'

She flushed and walked round the bed, sinking down

on it. Nick watched her, his brows level. Claire looked
at the tea machine, leaned over and switched it on, finding to her delight that it still worked. 'The electricity is
still on, anyway,' she said

'Not for long, I don't suppose,' Nick shrugged.

'At least we'll have a cup of tea,' she murmured.

He grinned. 'Very English, my darling.'

'I suppose you don't want one?' she retorted, her
chin lifting defiantly.

'I'd rather have a double Scotch,' he said wryly. 'But
I'll make do with tea.'

'Generous of you.' She went into the bathroom and
got her tooth mug, washed it out carefully and came
back with it just as the machine boiled. There was only
just enough tea for two and the milk powder just about
coloured it. Nick leaned over and dropped some sugar
lumps into her cup.

'I don't take sugar,' she said indignantly. 'Don't you
remember?'

'I remember,' he said drily. 'But you've had a shock,
you need it today.' He stood up and went into the bathroom. Claire heard the bath running and followed him
in bewilderment. 'What on earth are you doing?'

'Filling the bath with cold water,' he said. 'If they
turn off the water we may need it.'

She blenched. 'How long do you think we'll be here?'

He grimaced. 'Only until dark, I hope. Once the sun
sets we should be able to get along that corridor without the sniper seeing us, but I'm taking no chances. We
can go without food for days, but we need water.'

She went back into the bedroom and sat down on the
bed, drinking her tea with a sensation of luxury. So
much had happened since she awoke to the sound of

Nick hammering on the door that she felt as if she had been up for hours.

He wandered back into the room and drank his own tea, his hand curved around the mug. Putting it down after a moment, he said, 'Lie down and get some rest, Claire. You look shattered.'

'I'm fine,' she protested.

'Do as I tell you, there's a good girl,' he said patiently. 'I don't want you cracking up and we're here for hours.'

She lay down, only then realising how tense her body was, and trying consciously to relax it. Suddenly she thought of Andrew and sat up again. 'Andrew! What about Andrew?'

Nick shrugged. 'No idea. He has to look out for himself. You were my priority.'

'If nobody thought to warn him, he could walk out and get killed,' she said urgently.

'What do you suggest I do? Bang on the ceiling? Or risk my life out there trying to warn him?' Nick sounded angry. He looked at her grimly. 'Face it, Claire, there's no way we can reach him. In these situations you have to do what you can and forget what you can't.'

She sighed. 'I suppose you're right. What about your team? Philippa? Do they know?'

'Pip was the first to know,' he said. 'She heard the radio. You forget, she speaks Arabic. She warned us on the phone and I dressed and came straight up for you. I'm afraid I forgot bloody Andrew.'

'Why are you so angry?' she asked, baffled.

He sat down beside her on the bed, reaching for her with his good arm. 'I'll never have much time for the hotel whizz kid,' he said in barbed tones. 'I don't like the way he looks at you.'

'He doesn't . . .' she began.

'He damned well does,' Nick muttered, his mouth closing over hers. The first touch of his mouth worked the old magic. She surrendered without question, shaping herself in his arms, her face lifted ardently for his mouth, and her blood began to sing in her veins.

Nick moved his lips along the soft warm flesh of her neck, sending shivers down her back. 'At least I know I won't be interrupted this time,' he said grimly. 'There's something to be said for having gunmen posted outside each door. Bloody Andrew isn't bursting in here this time.'

Claire let her fingers slide down his chest, unbuttoning his shirt as they went, and he lifted his head to watch her, a little smile on the sensual mouth.

'You'll have to come home with me now,' she said happily. 'You can't stay out here with a bullet wound in your arm.' She pushed her face against his bare skin, sighing, 'Darling . . .'

Nick rubbed his chin against the top of the black head. 'No more lies or half truths between us, Claire,' he said quietly. 'I'm not leaving, bullet wound or no bullet wound.'

She lay still. Her happiness dissolved. The green eyes lifted to search his hard face. 'You can't mean it!'

'I could have lied to you,' he said in flat tones. 'I was badly tempted to, but I didn't. Claire, this is my job.'

'To throw your life away? For what?' She pushed him away and sat up, her body tense.

'For the hell of it,' he said, his jaw tight.

She looked at him bitterly. 'And what about me? I don't count, do I? You couldn't care less how I feel about it.'

'I care,' said Nick, his face unyielding. 'But if I walked out on this situation it would be the end of my career. I'm right on the spot and I have to take that story back if it kills me.'

'Which it probably will,' she said through white lips.

'It takes a lot to kill me,' he told her coolly.

'Someone just had a damned good try!'

'He grazed me,' Nick shrugged. 'I've had worse, I probably will again. It's part of the game.'

'Game? Is that how you see it?'

His brows flickered. 'The job, if you prefer. Some people are unlucky, they work just for the money. I work because it's what I love doing most of all.' His mouth went crooked. 'Apart from one other thing . . .' The blue eyes slid audaciously round at her. 'And nobody is going to pay me to do that.'

'Very funny, Nick,' she said coldly.

His smile died. 'I wasn't being funny,' he said.

'No,' she said, 'you weren't. I didn't even smile.'

He drew in his lower lip. 'Do I take it we're back to square one, with you hating me and a divorce on the agenda?'

'A divorce is the only answer, I see that now,' she said tensely, turning away from him.

He laughed harshly. 'Predictable little bitch, aren't you? But if you think I'm spending a day stuck in a bedroom with you and acting like a little wooden gentleman, you can think again, my darling.'

'Don't touch me!' she snapped, moving to evade the long hand as it snaked out for her.

'Damn you, my lovely little neurotic,' he muttered, yanking her back towards him roughly. 'I want you and I'm going to have you.'

'What makes you think you've any right to lay a finger on me?' she burst out bitterly. 'You intend to walk out on me after today, yet you still feel free to take anything you like!'

'That's right, sweetheart,' he said with cold emphasis. 'I'm taking everything I can while I've got the chance. After the divorce I'll have a few memories, anyway.'

'Nasty ones, I promise you that,' she said, hating him so badly she wanted to shoot him herself.

'We'll see about that,' he told her, his lips twisting.

Claire struggled against him, yet unconsciously trying not to hurt his wounded arm, so that she had no chance at all as he slowly forced her down against the pillows. His whole weight came down to hold her there, an immobile prisoner, while the blue eyes flickered over her flushed, angry face.

'I hate you,' she whispered. 'I don't want you to touch me.'

'I don't give a damn what you want,' he said, his voice harsh. 'It's what I want that's occupying my mind right now.'

'What a surprise!' she flung. 'What you want always has been the first priority.'

His eyes glinted. 'Not always,' he retorted. 'When we first met, I had a devil of a struggle stopping myself from taking you to bed that first night.'

'What makes you think I'd have let you?' she asked coldly.

He grinned. 'Swear to me you didn't want me, darling,' he taunted.

She bitterly wished she could. Instead, she asked icily, 'Did you make an exception for me? How gracious!'

Nick's lips curled. 'Are you accusing me of promiscuity now, you little scold?'

'How many others have there been in the past year?' she demanded. 'Or can't you remember?'

'I remember very clearly,' he drawled. 'I have total recall for things like that.'

Her nostrils flared jealously. 'I see,' she said between her teeth. 'Are you the type who doesn't tell?'

'Naturally,' he murmured, watching her between his dark lashes. 'You didn't want details, did you?'

'I don't want to hear a solitary thing,' she lied, burning with angry bitterness.

'Your eyes are greener than ever,' he said silkily, his hard lips curving in a teasing smile.

She lapsed into silence, her eyes averted. Nick continued to watch her without moving for a moment, then his hand moved to her cheek, stroking the soft flushed skin. She felt a quiver run over her and was furious with herself for reacting.

'Get your hands off me!' she hissed.

He bent his head very slowly, and her heart began a wild crescendo. His mouth silkily caressed her cheek, slid behind her ears and then made a sensuous descent along her throat. He undid her jacket and then her blouse. She felt heavily lethargic, unable to move to stop him. His mouth began to tease her, brushing over her bare shoulders and down the shadowy hollow between her white breasts.

'Don't Nick,' she begged huskily, aware that her desire to deny him was rapidly being eroded.

'It's been hell without you,' he muttered against her warm skin. 'I'm starving for you, Claire.'

Her body trembled. Heat burned along her skin. She closed her eyes in total surrender and his mouth came down on hers, exploring the warm parted sweetness she offered him without hesitation. Her hands went round his neck, she clung, responding hungrily. It had been so long, but her body knew every response he needed, and their lovemaking had a dreamlike inevitability which totally anaesthetised her brain. She sighed under his mouth. 'Love me . . .'

'I intend to,' he said, half laughing, half violent. 'I've intended to ever since I set eyes on you again.'

She half stirred at that, her resentment coming back, but Nick refused to allow her to resist. His hands moved over her hungrily.

'God knows how I've stayed away from you,' he muttered, the blue eyes flashing over her white body. 'I've thought of nothing else but this since the day you walked out.' His voice hardened, his jaw grew taut. 'How could you do that to me, Claire? You put me through hell. I couldn't keep my mind on my job for the first time in my life.'

'Well, at least I accomplished something,' she said in bitterness, staring at the hard sensual face above her. His eyes burnt down at her, his mouth violent.

'At times I hated you,' he muttered through those tightly controlled lips.

'I hated you,' she said, her bones contracting at the long look of the blue eyes.

A peculiar smile quivered over his face. 'And when I walked into that dining-room and saw your back, I felt as if I'd been kicked in the stomach.'

She remembered turning and looking at him, feeling herself drop through a hole in the world, all her hostility towards him wrenched away in the first sight of him. 'Yes,' she said. 'Yes.' He had looked so cool and controlled, his expression sardonic, yet she had known all the time that he was undergoing the same upheaval as herself. There had been so much between them, a whole world of passion and need, and one could not throw that away without throwing part of oneself away with it. Since they parted she had been incomplete, half dead, and she shuddered at the prospect of being the same way again.

Nick's eyes read the thoughts passing through her head. There was a silence between them, then his hand framed her face, cupping her chin in his warm palm.

'Has there been anyone else, Claire?' he asked casually, but she heard the echo of a deeper emotion behind the question.

In the beginning, she might have lied in self-protection, but now she merely shook her head.

His mouth lifted at the corners, his eyes deepened to a blinding blue. 'A whole year without a man? Tough, darling.' The smile was brilliant with charm.

'Did you think there was?' she asked wryly.

'I wasn't certain about Knight,' he admitted. 'Jealousy is a barbaric emotion and I don't enjoy the taste of it, but if I'd really thought there was . . .' His voice trailed off, his face hard.

'What?' she asked, watching him.

The blue eyes narrowed. 'I'd have killed him,' he shrugged, and beneath the coolness of the answer she read much more than the tone admitted.

'What typical male effrontery,' she said, her cheeks flushing. 'Why should there be two standards, one for you and one for me? You've admitted that there were other women for you.'

'Jealous, Claire?' he asked, his smile intent.

Her eyes blazed, as green as grass. 'You know very well I am!'

He gave a soft groan and the dark head bent. 'There hasn't been anyone else but you, Claire, since the day I met you,' he said thickly, then his mouth came down and she met it hungrily, her arms winding round his neck, her fingers running into the thick dark hair.

His mouth blazed into consuming demand, the strong hands roving over her, sending wild quivers of pleasure along her nerves. She wanted him so badly that she could have cried.

When the voice penetrated her brain she thought she was imagining it and shook her head dazedly, a frown on her face. Nick stiffened and sat up, pushing her away. The deep absorption of their lovemaking seemed to fall away from him and he was abruptly intent. As tense as a trapped animal, he sprang off the bed and moved to the door. The voice came again, yelling her name.

'Andrew,' she said, a hand at her mouth. She ran towards the door, calling back frantically, 'Andrew, don't come down here! There's a sniper on the mosque!'

Nick shot her an odd look. She was white with fear, her green eyes enormous.

'Keep away from the door,' he said tightly. 'Stand well back. I'm going to open it. If your stupid boyfriend makes a dash for it he may need some cover.'

Claire barely heard him, shaking with alarm. He gave her another look, then pushed her carelessly out of the way, throwing her back into the room. The door opened and a bullet whined in the silence.

'Keep away from here!' Nick shouted, his lean body

level with the doorframe to avoid presenting a target to the gunman.

There was a little silence. 'I've got a rifle,' Andrew shouted back. 'Stay where you are until you hear me shooting. I'm going to try to pin him down long enough to get you out!'

Nick's mouth twisted and he shot Claire another hard look. 'Right,' he yelled back.

'Sure there's only one of them?' Andrew demanded.

'On the mosque,' Nick called. 'Give us two minutes, then start shooting.'

Claire pressed a hand to her mouth. Nick turned and looked at her in cool contemplation. 'Think you can make it?'

She licked dry lips. 'Your arm,' she said irrelevantly. 'It's bleeding again—I can see the blood on the bandage. You must have banged it.'

He swore flatly. 'To hell with my arm! Claire, if Knight keeps that sniper occupied can you run along the corridor with me? You won't panic?'

'You might get killed,' she said, her lips shaking.

'I'll try to cover you as much as possible,' he told her. 'When Knight starts shooting, we're going out, and we're going to run like hell. Try to keep your body turned at an angle as you run and dodge about as much as you can, weave in and out . . . it makes it more difficult to keep a line on you.' He was white under his tan, his blue eyes flinty.

She nodded, beginning shakily to tidy her clothes. Nick moved to her and his lean face was shadowed as he helped her. His lips twisted. 'I might have known bloody Andrew would break it up between us, gunman or no gunman,' he said derisively. The blue eyes flickered bitterly. 'You were wrong about him wanting Pip, weren't you? He wants you enough to risk his life for you.' He looked at her unsmilingly. 'I'll give him this, the swine has guts.'

She winced, looking past him at the open door. 'Do you think he's really risking his life?' Her skin felt chilled. She thought of Andrew out there in a sniper's rifle sights and her lips trembled. 'Nick, if he gets killed . . .'

He read the look in her dilated eyes, his face cold. 'Yes, Claire, if he gets killed?'

She covered her face with her hands. 'Oh, God, why did we have to come out here just at this moment?'

Nick's hands closed over her shoulders, holding her against his chest. She trembled, leaning against him.

The sound of firing broke in upon them. Nick caught her hand and pulled her through the door. 'Run like blazes,' he ordered through stiff lips, keeping her on the right side of him, away from the windows.

CHAPTER SEVEN

SHE did not dare to glance across his protective body at the brilliant floor-length plate glass windows. The whine of bullets, the splintering sound as they hit the windows at the end of the corridor, the sickening thuds as they entered the plaster of ceiling and wall, seemed to fill her eardrums. The time seemed endless as they ran, weaving from side to side. She saw Andrew at the far end, his body tucked to one side as he fired out of the final window. As she focused on him, a bullet whizzed past his ear and he jerked away.

They were almost there when Nick caught her round the waist and flung her head first on the floor, his body close to her. 'We'll have to crawl the rest of the way,' he muttered. 'Keep your head well down.'

Claire found she was sweating, her blouse sticking to her heated skin, her face damp with beads of perspiration. Reaching the safety of the wall leading to the elevator she tremblingly stood up, with Nick's hands holding her, and leaned against the wall, her breath hurting in her lungs.

Andrew turned away from the window, propping up his rifle against the wall, and came to her. He looked down at her anxiously. 'All right?'

She nodded, too breathless to speak.

He stared for another second or two, then with a shaken gesture put his arms around her and held her against his body, his hand moving over her hair. 'My

God, I thought you might be dead,' he said heavily.

She was too distraught to move for a moment, grateful for his courage and kindness. She leant against him, her eyes closing. He was so large and comforting, the warmth of his body coming through his shirt. The human contact was balm and solace after her run along that death trap of a corridor. She had thought as she began to run that she might see Nick gunned down in front of her eyes. He had been using his own body to cover her, and that had been a bitter moment. She had always been so terrified that he would be killed, but for her to be the cause of his death would have been soul-destroying.

'Hadn't we better get out of here?' Nick asked tightly from behind her.

Andrew sounded wry. 'You're right, we haven't got much time. That's why I came up here. Pip and I guessed you must be holed up here—we spotted the sniper outside, and worked out that you'd be waiting for darkness to make a run for it. But the evacuation is due to take place at sunset off the Mulei beach. We have to get there under our own steam now, so the sooner we get away the better.'

'Where did you get the rifle?' Nick asked.

Andrew had released Claire now. She stood, her face very pale, staring at the wall, suffering from shock.

Andrew laughed, sounding exultant, as if he were actually enjoying himself. 'One of the rebels was shot down outside the hotel, and I went out and got his rifle.'

Nick surveyed him, eyebrows lifted. 'Quite a guy, aren't you?' He sounded drily complimentary.

Claire's widening eyes focused on Andrew's shoes and trouser legs. 'Andrew, there's blood on you . . . are you hurt?'

He shook his head. 'There's been quite a battle outside the hotel. Quite a few rebels lying out there—I had a quick look to see if I could do anything for them, but there wasn't a thing anyone could do. I must have got some blood on my clothes then.'

She winced. 'You might have been killed yourself, going out there like that . . . you shouldn't have done it!'

His brown eyes smiled at her. 'Did you expect me to leave you behind? I had to come and get you.'

'Shall we move?' Nick asked coolly.

Andrew grabbed up his rifle. 'The others are waiting downstairs in the basement—too dangerous in the foyer. Come on, we have to use the service stairs. The others are too dangerous—too many windows.'

As they made their way down the narrow, uncarpeted service stairs, Nick asked quietly, 'How is Philippa?'

'Fine,' Andrew said. 'I had the hell of a job stopping her from coming up with me.'

'How *did* you stop her?' Nick asked wryly. 'Knowing Pippa, it would have taken considerable persuasion.'

'I told her she would be more of a hindrance than a help,' Andrew admitted. 'How could I concentrate on what I had to do if I had to keep one eye open for her?'

Nick grimaced. 'What did she say?'

'Nothing pleasant,' Andrew confessed ruefully.

Claire was sick with misery. Now that she and Nick were out of the bedroom, the time was fast approaching when she would have to go, leaving him behind her, knowing now just what dangers he was facing. An ache began inside her. She felt like screaming out her fear, her love, but she went on down the stairs, somehow controlling her features into a quiet mask. She did not want his last memory of her to be bitter. She would not allow any of her emotions to show on her face from now on, she would act out the role he appeared to wish her to play.

Her hurrying feet skidded on the uncarpeted stairs and she slipped. Both Nick and Andrew moved to catch her. She could not bear to have Nick touch her; it would be too bitter-sweet. Her slender body swerved slightly away from him into Andrew's waiting hands, and he supported her, his face concerned. 'You're pale. Are you O.K.?'

She nodded speechlessly, straightening.

As she moved on she caught Nick's hard blue stare. It was blank. She looked away quickly, compressing her lips. If she even spoke to him she might start to beg. Andrew's presence would not inhibit her once she opened her lips. She knew she would break down, cry, plead, make a fool of herself.

She had not broken down when she left him last time; she had been too worn out by sleepless nights and cold anger. This time it was worse. She was going to leave him in terrible danger, and she had failed hopelessly to persuade him to come with her. She had to face the fact that his job came first; she ran it a poor second. For the moment she would not let herself dwell on that —it hurt too much. For the present, she only had one aim—to preserve a calm exterior in front of him at all costs. She would not let him see how badly he had hurt her when he refused to come with her to safety.

They emerged in the basement and a moment later the rest of the TV team were surrounding them, grinning, slapping Nick and Andrew on the back. Their attitude to Andrew, she noted wryly, had changed drastically. His act of heroism had impressed them.

'He wouldn't even let any of us help,' Wazi said to Nick. 'There was only one rifle which was suitable for that distance, and he said we would merely give the sniper some target practice.' He grinned, his black eyes bright. 'We were relieved to hear it, I can tell you.'

Nick grinned back at him. 'Yeah, I know what a coward you are, you liar,' he said affectionately. He glanced at Andrew. 'Wazi saved my life on a couple of occasions,' he explained.

'It was my job,' Andrew said flatly, shrugging. 'I'm a trained shot.'

Nick raised a brow enquiringly. 'Rifle club?'

'He's won medals for it,' Wazi informed him lightly.

'And Claire was my responsibility,' Andrew said calmly, meeting Nick's blue eyes.

There was a short silence. Nick's expression was unreadable. Philippa glanced at him, her face concerned.

'As Andrew's secretary,' her voice offered. 'He brought her here, so he feels responsible for her.'

'Of course,' Nick said smoothly. 'When are we moving?'

Claire looked at him then, her heart leaping. 'Are you coming after all?' she asked hoarsely.

He flickered a look at her. 'I'll see you on that ship,' he said levelly, then the blue eyes swivelled towards Andrew. 'How do we get out of here?'

'There's a service entrance at the side,' Andrew told him. 'It's under cover to the road, thank God. They got the other guests out that way hours ago. We waited for you two.'

'We couldn't do a programme without our talking head,' Wazi told Nick teasingly. 'I offered to do the chat instead, but I was turned down.'

Nick grinned briefly at him. 'How do we get from the hotel to the beach?'

They all looked at Andrew. 'Two chances,' he said crisply. 'There's a van we could take, but we run the risk of snipers in that—or we can take a long walk, which might be safer, but will take much longer. Up to the rest of you which way we go.'

'There's no need for the whole team to go,' said Nick, fingering his chin. 'Safer to stay here, frankly. I'll see Andrew and Claire to the beach.'

'I'm coming with you,' Philippa said quickly. 'You can't run that gauntlet on your own twice, Nick.'

'Me, too,' Wazi said lightly.

Nick shook his head at them both. 'Stay put. I'll be back.'

'I'm coming,' Philippa repeated, her jaw obstinate.

Andrew had listened impassively. Now he turned on her and snapped bitingly, 'For God's sake, you stupid bitch, don't you know when you're not wanted?'

She whitened, biting her lower lip.

Nick's face grew black with temper. 'What do you do for an encore?' he asked Andrew savagely. 'Kick old ladies?'

Andrew's eyes hardened. 'I'm only telling her the obvious. She's adding to our risks, not diminishing them, if she comes with us. Three of us have to face the journey. Why add to the number?'

Nick turned to Philippa, his shoulders rueful. 'He's right, Pip. Stay here, please, for my sake.'

She turned away, her body stiff. 'Very well,' she said in a low voice.

Claire felt pain eating at her insides. Nick's concern and gentleness to Philippa, his apparent acceptance that she would be staying in Keravi with him, stung her jealousy into hot life. Philippa would be with him while she was being taken away to safety to wait for the news of his death or at the best his serious injury. She had no part in his life, his real life, which was here, with the rest of the team, working beside them every day, sharing their lives. He might love her, he might desire her, but he would not give up anything for her. She was an occasional pleasure, a plaything, a possession. Even had she not left him, their marriage would have had no existence in the real world—he would have been a brief visitor, a lover, who dropped in out of the blue without warning and left again the same way, like the swallows, winging their way across continents, appearing and disappearing in season.

'Ready, then?' Andrew asked.

She nodded without looking up. She heard the team wish them good luck. Philippa moved closer and said quietly, 'Take care, Claire.'

She looked at her dully, wishing she dared to reply, 'Take care of Nick for me', but she could only say in return, 'And you.' Her eyes flickered over Philippa, and she wished vainly she could hate her, even dislike her, but Philippa was a very nice girl, and she liked and admired her. She just envied her the courage, brains and strength which made her a suitable companion for Nick.

They went out through the service corridor, a drab hollow tube painted metallic grey, which led out to the road. Andrew positioned himself in the shelter of a flowering hedge by the gate while he stared along the road, his rifle just poking out. There was not a sound, not a movement. The white dust was stained red in places. The windowless white walls of the houses stared down blankly at them. Andrew's eyes flicked over the flat roofs, but there was no sign of anyone moving.

'You go first, Nick,' he said over his shoulder.

When Nick had run zigzagging into an alley some hundred feet away, Andrew told Claire to go, and covered her while she ran, his eyes moving restlessly.

Nick looked at her quickly as she joined him in the shelter of a car, abandoned by its owner, the windscreen splintered into a million crystallised particles by a bullet. He was crouching down beside it, his body tense. The blue eyes stripped her face.

'Don't be frightened,' he said tautly.

'I'm not,' she said. She did not care if she was killed. She could only see Nick's death approaching like an express train which would some day crush her life.

His mouth twisted. 'Of course, Andrew's there to protect you,' he jeered.

She read sarcasm in the remark and looked at him angrily. 'He's being fantastic,' she said in sharp tones.

'He should get a medal,' Nick agreed, but his eyes were dark. 'Does it flatter you to know he's doing it all for you?'

She flushed at that. 'Andrew has a strong sense of responsibility.'

Nick laughed shortly. 'He's crazy about you, you mean.'

Andrew came skimming into position beside them and Nick's mouth snapped tight. There was a flush of enjoyment on Andrew's hard face, a gleam in the brown eyes. 'Next stretch,' he told Nick. 'Go for the corner of that house up there . . . good cover as it turns.'

Nick nodded and ran. Claire followed, when she saw

him safely pressed into the rounded curve of the wall, out of sight of everywhere but a flat roof opposite. She reached him, breathing hard. Nick kept his eyes on the roof, his profile averted from her. Suddenly a figure moved there and Nick forced her down on her face, his body covering her. A shot whined and plaster dust showered down on them, whitening Nick's black hair. Another shot followed it almost instantly. She heard a choked cry and a crashing sound, the slither of feet and then another crash in the road opposite. She lifted her head, but Nick forced it down again, his hand covering her hair.

'For God's sake, lie still, you little fool!' he snapped. 'There may be another one!'

She lay still, trembling violently. Nick's hard body pressed her down and despite the peril of their situation she felt her pulses beating wildly.

Andrew's feet thudded to a halt beside them. His voice was light with excitement. 'You can get up now. I got the poor devil and there isn't another one.'

Nick's body lifted from her, then he helped her up, his blue eyes cool on her face. She instinctively turned to look across at the still body on the dusty road, but Nick moved between her and the sight, shaking his head. 'You'd only have nightmares,' he said tersely.

Nick set off again, ducking and weaving into shelter, and Claire followed, her heart shaking inside her. They saw nothing living. The houses were shuttered and barred. Even the dogs were out of sight. The white-walled little streets lay empty and dreaming in the hot sunlight. The air of peace seemed at variance with the sounds they could hear from the centre of the town—the constant flash and thud of arms, the whine of bullets, the crash of mortars landing. Little columns of smoke wound like grey scarfs into the blue sky. Occasionally one caught the glitter of light from an explosion as it was reflected off the plate glass of the new hotels.

The beach area was comparatively tranquil. There were few key positions in this part of the town. Most of the inhabitants had locked themselves indoors and the foreign guests had all been evacuated by now.

They scrambled down the last alley leading to the Mulei beach and saw the lines of people waiting there. The afternoon had worn down to a purple dusk. The light was fast fading and the sight of a British ship standing offshore made Claire feel slightly sick with relief.

Boats were transferring the waiting evacuees from shore to ship, ferrying them rapidly in those patient line-ups, while British officials quietly checked the nationality and papers of each. It almost made Claire smile to see the order and calm which prevailed. The people might have been lining up for a bus, instead of waiting to be carried out of possible peril.

When they came down on to the sand, one of the officials approached Andrew with a welcoming smile. He recognised him from a previous visit.

'So you got here, sir? Great.' A thin, fair young man in a crisp white shirt, he glanced at Claire and Nick enquiringly. 'British?'

'This is my secretary, Miss Thorpe,' said Andrew, his arm going round her shoulders to pull her forward.

'Your papers, Miss Thorpe?' the young man asked, smiling

She bit her lip. 'At the hotel,' she stammered. 'In my suitcase . . . I couldn't bring them . . .'

'I'll vouch for her,' said Andrew, his voice commanding. 'She's worked for me for a year.' He scratched his chin, a grin on his face. 'In fact, I've got a photo of her at our last office party here.' He brought out a wallet and extracted it, showing it to the young man. Against an office background she stood with Andrew, laughing. On the other side of her stood Sir Joseph Lang, the company chairman, a famous international figure. The official looked at him, grinned. 'Sir Joseph,' he recognised. 'You keep imposing company, Miss Thorpe. You'll have to clear this at the other end. Just get on the ship now. We'll sort it out, don't worry.'

He turned from her to Nick. 'Your papers, sir?'

Nick was watching Andrew return the photograph to his wallet and put it away once more. His face was expressionless, but his hard mouth was held in a straight line. He glanced at the official coolly. 'I'm not boarding,' he said without emphasis. 'I'm a journalist and I'll be staying on.'

The young man grimaced. 'That's inadvisable, sir, if you'll excuse me. Things could get very nasty here.'

Nick nodded. 'I realise that, thanks. I'm still staying.'

Claire trembled and Andrew looked down at her in sharp enquiry. Her green eyes met his gaze, a desperate misery in them. He put an arm round her and held her warmly. 'We'd better join that line-up before it gets any longer,' he said, glancing at Nick. 'Good luck, Waring. Don't take any risks.'

'Can I have that rifle?' Nick asked. 'I might find it handy on the way back.'

The young official had moved off now. Andrew handed over the rifle with a grin. 'Know how to handle it?' he asked.

Nick's head came up, the blue eyes sparked dangerously. 'Don't patronise me,' he said through his teeth.

Andrew stared, his brow lifted. 'I wasn't,' he said mildly. 'Just going to give you a few tips.'

'I'll manage,' Nick said shortly.

Andrew glanced down at Claire's white, averted face. 'Well . . .' he said slowly. 'I'll leave you two to say goodbye . . . don't be too long, Claire.'

He moved away and she stood, pointing her toe into the soft sand, her eyes fixed on the sea which was already darkening under the setting sun. The waves whispered up on to the beach. The files of people talked in low tones behind them.

'You haven't a damn thing to say to me, have you, Claire?' Nick asked in a low voice, watching her.

'What is there to say that hasn't already been said?' she asked quietly.

He laughed harshly. 'Not a thing,' he agreed. 'Get on the ship, Claire.'

She turned to go, her heart heavy. Nick muttered something under his breath and caught her shoulders, spinning her round to face him, his dark head bent to find her mouth, but she twisted her head away, evading him, too angry to care. He was deliberately throwing his life away and it did not matter to him that he was breaking her heart. She would not let him kiss her.

His hands clamped her head, crushing her cheekbones, fixing her face between the strong palms so that she could not move it. He stared down through the slow-falling dusk at her, his blue eyes flickering over the oval face, running from the green eyes to the soft mouth, their expression unreadable.

'The last time, Claire,' he said in a voice which

sounded icy. 'Surely you can kiss me for the last time?'

'No, I can't,' she said through lips which felt stiff.

'Too bad, you'll just have to grin and bear it,' he muttered in savagery, finding her mouth.

She tightened herself against him, her lips remaining shut under his, her body held tensely. Her refusal drove him to bitter reprisal. He forced his mouth down against hers, grinding her teeth against her lips, releasing the salt taste of blood into her mouth. His hands moved from her cheeks, forcing themselves savagely upward into the silky black hair, winding it around the long fingers, tugging at it to throw her head backward. Her body bent helplessly like a sapling in high winds, his hard limbs pressing against her. She struggled to pull away, but one of his hands detached itself from her hair and slid down her back, propelling her relentlessly towards him, pushing her in ruthless determination until she lay against him, unable to escape.

Under his cruel mouth her lips parted at last, to whisper, 'I hate you!'

He took advantage of the movement, forcing her to part them even further. She made no move to return his kiss, her whole being clenched in enmity. He lifted his head briefly to look into the angry, bitter green eyes. A wry grimace twisted his mouth.

'Goodbye, Claire,' he said in a muffled tone, then his mouth came down again, hungry, demanding, possessive, and she felt her own instinctive response clamouring for expression. She wanted to cling, to beg, to cry, but she shut her eyes and refused to think.

After what seemed to her an eternity, Nick released her and stepped back with one last, brief look from blue eyes which seemed oddly blank. Then he turned, picked up the rifle and walked away without another word, and her world seemed to shake and dissolve around her. She stared after his lean, departing figure desperately. Why had she refused to kiss him? she asked herself miserably. Why had she been so hard, so cold when she wanted nothing more than to cling and let him see how madly she loved him?

He had gone and she might never see him again alive. Her world would mean nothing to her without him, yet she had let him go without a word, a kiss.

'Claire, we must go,' Andrew said quietly at her shoulder.

She turned, unaware of the tears running blindingly down her white face, and Andrew made a soft exclamation, pulling her into his arms, his hand stroking the sleek dark hair.

'He'll be killed!' she wailed, shaking violently, so unsteady on her feet that she reached up and clung to Andrew's wide shoulders.

'No, no,' Andrew comforted, his hand moving down her hair. Over her head he stared at Nick's vanishing figure. Suddenly Nick turned and glanced back. One brief look at them, then he swung away and vanished into the town.

'We must get on that ship,' Andrew said gently. 'Pull yourself together, there's a good girl. You've been very brave until now. Let me see you smile again.'

He pushed her away from him kindly, wiped her wet face with a handkerchief and looked at her with sympathy. 'Don't fret over Nick. He's been through plenty of these situations before and he knows how to take care of himself. Journalists are like cats, they have nine lives.'

She drew herself up, her lips stiffly smiling. 'I'm fine now,' she said in a thready voice. 'It was the shock, I suppose.'

'We've all had a tough time today,' he agreed calmly.

'You've been marvellous, Andrew,' she said, smiling at him.

He flushed and grinned. 'Oh, I enjoyed some of it.'

Were all men slightly mad? she wondered, as she followed him into the snaking line-up for the boats. Both Andrew and Nick seemed to find something enjoyable about facing danger, as if they were frustrated boy scouts, looking for adventure in a drab world. They risked their lives gaily as if they were meaningless toys to be thrown away without a qualm. Claire thought about her father's mad quest for more and more speed, his reckless daring and gaiety. She remembered vividly for the first time how his eyes had danced with excitement before a race, how his whole face seemed to come alive with anticipation.

For years she had hated and blamed him for the bitter tangle he had made of his life, for the quarrels with her mother, the tension in the house, his own death followed so shortly by her mother's suicide. Now for the first time Claire looked at her parents from outside, and she wondered bleakly if her mother had killed herself because she could not bear a world in which her husband did not exist. That thought had never occurred to her before. She had put her mother's suicide down to misery because of her unhappy marriage, but she could remember now other moments, when her mother had looked at her father with wild, adoring eyes, and she suddenly saw that as well as grief and fear there had been love between them, too.

Nick was right when he dismissed her mother's suicide as cowardly, but Claire felt, in a new impulse of sympathy, a sort of understanding for her mother's action. She had always despised her mother for what she did, secretly, but looking at it now she felt a wave of painful comprehension.

Later that night she leaned on the ship's rail, with Andrew standing silently beside her, staring back towards the vanishing coastline. The sky exploded from time to time in flashes of bright light. Against the soft purple of the sky were outlined the climbing fingers of the plate glass hotels, their dark outlines standing above the rest of the little town.

Somewhere in there, Nick was risking his life in the pursuit of his job. She felt a bitter certainty that she would never see him again, never feel his arms around her, taste his mouth on her own. She had rejected him on the beach. Under his passionate kiss she had stood like a stone statue. Now she was trembling with hunger and desire, her green eyes filled with desperation, and she had no way of telling him that she would have crawled on her hands and feet through fire to say she loved him.

CHAPTER EIGHT

IT took Andrew just a few hours to sort out the muddle over Claire's lack of documentation. He left her at the hotel at which they had booked in, went out, his chin stuck out belligerently, and came back walking with his light tread, a grin on his face. Andrew liked to win. He had a competitive spirit, a passion for the struggle and for the pleasure of victory at the end of it.

He came to her room and she let him in, her eyes feverish in her white face. 'Any news?' The words burst out as if she could not help it, and indeed she couldn't—she had thought of nothing else since they arrived.

'I've got you clearance,' he said, misunderstanding her. His brown eyes glinted. 'I gave them hell until they pulled all the stops out for you. They were doing the usual wooden official act until I kicked up a fuss, but I know a few people, and they were soon moving.'

She smiled politely, her indifference masked. 'Thank you, Andrew.' He deserved her gratitude. He had done so much for her, not merely in coming up to get her and Nick out of that room, but ever since, too. He had been gentle, considerate and sympathetic on the boat, and since they arrived at the hotel he had been tirelessly working on her behalf to get her home safely to England, although any other boss might well have gone ahead, leaving her to wait for her papers and make her own way home.

He looked satisfied. He liked to know his victories were appreciated, although she knew that he would have worked as hard without praise, because Andrew always had to win, and hated muddle and officialdom, the bureaucratic lethargy of Whitehall.

She paused, to give him time to listen to her, then said again, 'Any news from Keravi?'

He glanced at her sharply. 'I'm sorry,' he said, shaking his head. 'Not a word.'

Something in his voice made her doubt him, and she stared at him probingly, her hands clenching. 'Andrew?' The shake in her voice made her appeal clear.

His straight mouth levelled further. 'Just rumours,' he said in a tone intended to sooth. 'Nothing certain.'

'What sort of rumours?'

'God knows,' he shrugged, turning away. 'They conflict.'

'Tell me, Andrew,' she broke out, turning her nails into her hot palms. 'I'm not a child!'

'One version is that the Sheik has got control again and is busy rounding up the rebels,' he said quietly. 'The other is that the rebels have won and are liquidating the loyal troops.'

Claire closed her eyes. Terror split the dark sky of her mind. 'They don't know which is the truth?'

'They only know the radio is silent and no planes have left or landed since the coup began,' he told her gently. 'Silence is better than it sounds—if the rebels still held the radio they would be boasting over it loud and clear.'

She sat down on her bed heavily, her hands knitted in her lap. Andrew came over to her, sat down and put a hand over the tortuous fingers. 'Stop beating your head against a brick wall,' he murmured. 'It does no good, Claire. We have to keep a sane view of the situation.'

'I shan't be able to sleep until I know he's out of there,' she said miserably.

'Then the sooner we get home the better,' he said. 'I've booked seats on the next flight to London. Pack as soon as you can.'

'I've nothing to pack,' she reminded him dully.

He grinned. 'True—I'd forgotten.' The brown eyes swept over her slim figure in the olive green suit. 'You manage to look ravishing all the same,' he said approvingly. 'Anyone would think you'd spent the last two days at a garden party instead of running the gauntlet of sniper fire and then a tough crossing on a rough boat.'

She smiled, her face relaxing a little. 'It always helps to be complimented,' she admitted wryly.

'Glad to be of service,' he grinned.

'What time is our plane?'

'Early hours, I'm afraid,' he told her ruefully. 'I took the first seats I could get. I thought you'd rather get home than sit around here waiting. I'd suggest you snatch a few hours sleep until we have to go to the airport. You must be worn out, poor girl.'

She sighed. 'I'm too tense to sleep.'

'You mustn't let it get you down, Claire,' he insisted. The brown eyes flickered over her again. 'Hungry?'

She shook her head.

Andrew's teeth worried his lower lip. 'All the same, I want you to eat something. You've barely touched a thing since we arrived.' He got up and went to the telephone beside the bed and rang room service, ordering a meal for two. As he replaced it, he glanced at her.

'You won't object if we eat up here?'

'I'd rather do that,' she said quickly. 'We might hear some news and I wouldn't want to hear it downstairs in public.' She might break down in front of strangers, and that would be hell.

He returned to her side, sinking down beside her, turning her white face towards him. 'I think you owe me some sort of explanation now, Claire. This marriage of yours . . . why all the secrecy?'

She sighed deeply, her shoulders shaking. 'It's a long story.'

'We've got plenty of time,' he said flatly. 'And I want to know.'

She looked down. 'Nick and I got married before I found out what sort of job he did . . . I knew I couldn't take that life, waiting all the time, expecting him to be killed. So we split up and I took the job with you. We'd never publicised our marriage and it was over so quickly that I almost didn't feel married at all. So I resumed my maiden name and I kept quiet about Nick.'

'You might have let me in on the secret,' he commented drily. 'I might have made a complete ass of myself over you.'

Colour swept up her face. Her eyes flickered to his face and away again quickly. 'If I'd thought there was any chance of that I would have told you,' she said.

'Thanks,' he said, his voice very dry.

There was a silence. 'I gather that you two have resolved your differences?' he asked.

She shook her head without a word.

'No?' Andrew sounded disbelieving. 'Come off it, Claire. He was very much acting the man in possession when I was around.'

She flushed deeper. 'That's Nick.'

'Possessive by instinct but not very faithful?' His voice had a sharp, cold tone now.

'It isn't quite like that,' she said vaguely. 'We still disagree about his job.'

Andrew considered her silently. She looked up and their eyes met. He said quietly, 'A man's work is a large part of his personality, Claire. Do you think you're wise?'

She was suddenly swept with misery. Turning away, she flung herself face down on the bed and wept into the pillow, her hands clenched by her sides. Andrew leaned over after a moment and lifted her into his arms, holding her comfortably as if she were a child, stroking her hair with one hand. The tears flooded down her face, ran into her mouth and down her throat. She was weeping for a complex tangle of reasons—she was terrified for Nick, she was guilty because she had rejected him on the beach, she was afraid that even if he came home safely he would never want to see her again.

Andrew put a hand beneath her chin and lifted her face towards him, then bent and kissed her gently, warmly, on her mouth. Claire closed her eyes, grateful for the comfort of that gesture.

Andrew's lips moved away for a few seconds, and she was about to smile gratefully at him, when they returned, their pressure harder, more demanding. She stiffened then, her eyes flying open, and pushed at his powerful chest, but he had both arms around her body and was immovable, his mouth coaxingly moving over hers.

'No, Andrew,' she protested, her voice muffled under his lips.

For another moment the warm mouth continued to press down against her lips, then it withdrew and Andrew stared into her eyes.

'No?' he asked her wryly. 'I thought you were giving me the green light at last, Claire. You had your eyes shut and you were smiling.'

She bit her lower lip. 'I misunderstood,' she said regretfully.

'What did you misunderstand?'

'I thought you were kissing me for comfort,' she said, her thoughts muddled.

'I was,' he said, smiling. 'Didn't it comfort you? I found it a pleasant pastime, myself.'

She laughed at that. 'Unwise, though,' she said, avoiding his gaze uncomfortably.

'Ah!' Andrew settled her on the bed and stood up. 'I'm sorry. I somehow had the impression your marriage was definitely over.'

'It is,' she agreed in flat tones.

'But I still get a red light?'

'I love him,' she said, her mouth crooked. 'I'm crazy about him.'

'Then you're a fool,' Andrew said with a grim look. 'If you want him, grab him before someone else does . . . like Philippa. She's there on the spot, waiting for him, Claire. Or don't you care?'

'Of course, I care,' she flared bitterly. 'But . . .'

'No buts,' said Andrew, his jaw tight. 'Make up your mind, you little idiot—either you take him or you forget him. There's no middle road except one which leads to madness. Keep fending him off and shutting yourself away from the rest of mankind at the same time, and you'll end up climbing the walls. We all need somebody, and you more than most, Claire. You're the ultra-feminine type.' His mouth twisted. 'Take Philippa, for instance . . . easy to imagine her getting by without a man to cling to! She's got guts, I'll grant her that. I was impressed by her coolness when the trouble broke out. She came up to my room to get me out of there, you know. We got out just in time. A bullet whizzed past her head and nearly took it off, and she didn't bat an eyelid.'

Claire stared at him, her face surprised. So Philippa had got him out of his room! 'It was nice of her to run that risk for you,' she said softly.

He flushed. 'Yes.' His mouth tightened. 'She'd have done the same for you if Nick hadn't been there to do it.'

'I still don't think she cares for Nick in any way,' she said very carefully.

'He's an attractive devil,' Andrew admitted, his voice hard. 'They understand each other. I've never heard her raise her voice to him. She seems to understand him before he opens his mouth.' He looked at her thoughtfully. 'That's one sign of love, Claire. Don't you think?'

She blenched. 'I suppose so.' It was true. She had noticed how closely Philippa seemed to follow Nick's thoughts, reading his mind, her eyes smiling at him.

It had hurt her to know that Nick calmly accepted Philippa's right to stay in Keravi with him, although he had bustled her on to that ship, waving goodbye to her almost without regret. Claire's mouth turned down at the edges, her green eyes glowed with bitterness. Nick knew she was no fit wife for him. She would always shrink in terror when she was faced with the dangers of his job, while Philippa acted quietly and coolly, more like a man than a woman. Philippa belonged with Nick. They were the same sort of person.

The floor waiter arrived with their meal, and they ate it in a silence shadowed by their unspoken thoughts. Andrew glanced at her as they finished. 'Now, try to get some sleep, Claire. You look half dead, you know.'

'Thanks,' she muttered, grimacing.

He smiled wearily. 'I feel like death myself, don't worry. The last few days have been very trying.'

She took his advice and rested for some time on her bed, her eyes shut, her body limp, but images kept disturbing her thought, breaking her out of the faint ring of sleep, dragging her back to an anguished awareness. She had refused to soften towards Nick on the beach when he kissed her, and she was paying for it now, as she faced the fact that she might never see him again. Whatever it cost her, she should have put her personal grief aside to say goodbye to him. If anything happened to him, she knew she would be haunted for the rest of her life by having been so cold and hard at that moment.

She and Andrew flew back to England that night and arrived back in typical English weather, the rain pouring down in dark torrents, the sky showing the colour of molten lead.

Andrew's car took her to her apartment before dropping him back at the office. Just before they parted she said shyly, 'Would you like me to resign now, Andrew? Or shall I wait until you can find a replacement?'

He gave her a quick, unsmiling look. 'I don't want you to leave, Claire.'

She looked uncertain, biting her lip. 'Are you sure? Don't you think it would be best after . . .'

'We work well together,' he said flatly. 'It would be

stupid to ruin our working relationship just because of a few days in Keravi.'

She half laughed. His calm common sense was unanswerable. A few days in Keravi, she thought. Yes, that was all it was—a few strange days which bore no relationship to what had gone before or what would probably follow afterwards.

Andrew's brown eyes probed her oval face. 'Well?' he demanded, his voice flat.

She gave him a wry smile. 'Just as you like, Andrew.'

'You enjoy your job, don't you?' he asked.

'Yes,' she agreed, 'I enjoy it.' She had done until now, but her brain asked her secretly whether she would go on doing so after all that had happened. The year with Andrew had been a sanctuary, a hiding place, where the misery of her marriage to Nick could not reach her. Now things had changed, despite Andrew's quiet voice and face. She and Andrew had worked together as strangers. They knew a lot about each other now, and their relationship must change, by the nature of things.

When she had left him she tried to exorcise her thoughts by dwelling on purely practical problems, moving around her apartment, her face blank, but she felt anxiety like a cloud around her head.

Andrew had insisted that she take the following day off to rest, so she spent the time in quiet occupations, cleaning, shopping, doing her laundry. It was impossible to stop her mind from dwelling on the subject of Nick, and she was glad to return to work on the day after; it would at least give her something to think about. Andrew was a dynamic boss. He left one no time to sit about brooding.

Oddly, she found that the intimacy which had grown between them during their trip had sent down deep roots. They had always worked well together, but now there was an added dimension in that partnership. She had always respected Andrew. Now, remembering his courage and determination during their escape from the hotel, she found herself admiring him far more, and clearly Andrew's attitude towards her had changed as much. He spoke to her more confidentially, he treated her less as a piece of office furniture and more as a person whom she liked and trusted.

The days passed very slowly. Claire found herself constantly turning on the radio, listening for any scraps of news, but the reports out of Keravi were muddled and difficult to interpret. Andrew shook his head over her pale face and glazed green eyes. 'You're letting yourself get into a state over this,' he said disapprovingly.

'If only I knew something!' she whispered, her fingers locked together.

He stared at her, his mouth grim, then turned and walked out. Ten minutes later he came back and looked at her quietly. 'I've made some enquiries,' he said. 'The latest news is that it's quite definite that the rebellion has failed. The Sheik is busy mopping up the trouble-makers, but the airport will be opening again soon, so we should get more detailed news any day.'

She relaxed with a long sigh. Andrew stared at her without speaking, then turned and left again without another word. Claire was grateful to him for having gone to so much trouble on her behalf, but a faint warning note sounded in her mind. She did not want Andrew to get too involved with her. How did one make that plain without being ridiculous? She might be wildly wrong and he would think her very conceited.

Two nights later Nick's hard, dark face appeared on the television screen and she gasped, leaning forward to listen intently, her eyes shimmering with love. Against the all too familiar background of the blue sky, glass and concrete of the holiday area, Nick spoke in that terse, rapid voice about the failed coup, but she barely heard a word he said; her heart and mind were too active absorbing every tiny thing about him. Beneath the bronze skin she thought she detected a tinge of pallor, and there was a bitter pull to his level, sensual mouth.

When the report ended and his face disappeared from the screen, she lay back, breathing deeply, trying to control the trembling which had spread through her body. The physical relief was overwhelming. She ached with the lift of the tension which had dominated her for so many days.

When the telephone began to shrill she moved to it slowly, forcing herself to lift one foot after another, as if she were suffering from an illness.

'Claire?'

She recognised Andrew's voice and broke into muffled speech. 'Did you see him?'

There was a silence. 'Yes,' said Andrew. 'I rang to see if you had caught the news. So. All's well that ends well.'

'Yes,' she said breathlessly.

'Right,' said Andrew. 'Goodnight, Claire.'

For a few seconds she thought she had misheard, but the phone had gone dead in her hand and she could only hear the burr of the tone which told her he had hung up. Slowly she put the phone down and went back to her chair, her face bothered.

Andrew had sounded odd—there was no doubt about that. She frowned. Perhaps she should have resigned her job, after all.

That Friday, just as she was finishing work, he wandered into her office and regarded her thoughtfully. 'You need a good break. Why not go down to visit your family in Suffolk? Some sea air might put the colour back into your face? Take a few days off. I can manage.'

She was tempted and smiled at him gratefully. 'Thank you, I would enjoy that. If you're sure you can manage without me?'

The brown eyes reflected a sardonic smile and colour came into her cheeks. 'Oh, I think I can just about cope without you, Claire,' he murmured drily.

She did not quite like the way he said it. There was a deliberate inflection which worried her. Looking down, she said, 'Then thank you, I think I will.'

Dad was astonished and delighted to see her when she arrived at the cottage. She had had no time to let him know she was coming since he had been out when she rang several times the previous evening. She knew he kept a key under a flowerpot in the greenhouse, however, so she had known she could get in if the cottage was empty when she arrived, so she had come anyway.

After he had hugged her, exclaiming at the surprise, she sat down in the kitchen with a mug of coffee and poured out her story.

Dad listened, eyes curious, his face expressing dismay and shock as her story progressed. 'Poor Nick,' he commented, when she had ended.

She stared at him, bristling. 'Poor Nick? He loves it all, the danger, the risk . . . it's the breath of life to him.' She had left out many details, particularly those of a more personal nature, such as her refusal to kiss Nick goodbye.

Dad looked at her, scratching his wiry chin. 'He must have been out of his mind when he realised what you'd got mixed up in,' he said softly. 'You were in terrible danger, Claire. You might have been killed.'

She shrugged that thought away. At no time during those hectic hours had she really feared for her own life, only for Nick's, and she did not imagine Nick had ever been afraid for her, either. 'Nick made sure I got out of it,' she said angrily. 'He couldn't get me on that ship fast enough.'

'I can imagine,' Dad said wryly. 'As I said, poor Nick.'

She looked at him bitterly. 'He stayed, though, although he was wounded.'

'It's his job,' said Dad, shaking his head. 'Can't you try to understand that, darling? Nick puts a lot of himself into his job. Some men need that sort of risk, God knows why. You're asking the impossible if you ask him to change. The man you fell in love with is the same man who gets a kick out of roving the world from trouble spot to trouble spot. If you had a dog, you wouldn't expect it to mew, would you?'

She grinned involuntarily at the down-to-earth question. 'Oh, you always take his side in arguments!'

'There are no sides,' Dad said soberly. 'I love you, darling, and I hate to see you wasting your chances of happiness this way.'

'Why have you been seeing him during the last year?'

she burst out. 'He told me he'd been down here, that you'd let him read my letters . . . why did you do that? You knew how I felt.'

Dad eyed her ruefully. 'I felt sorry for him,' he explained. His mouth quivered. 'I waited for years for your mother, Claire, and I know how it can hurt to be shut out.'

She softened at that, her eyes tender. 'I'm sorry,' she said, giving him a kiss. 'I know you did it for the best. I just wish . . .'

'What, Claire?' he asked gently.

'That I'd never met him,' she said miserably, tears welling into her eyes, then she jumped up and fled to her own little bedroom to cry on her bed, her slender body shaking.

Nothing had changed, she thought. Nick was still deeply involved with his job, risking his neck without thought, and he had no intention of changing either now or in the future. She had not changed, either. She was still racked by fear for him, unable to sleep or relax because she dreaded what news she might hear. What had happened in Keravi had been just what she could have expected to happen if she ever ran into him again. The desire he had showed her had only been what she should have anticipated. The passion she felt for him had not diminished during their year apart, so why should she have imagined that that basic, fundamental reaction between them should have meant anything? The lowest common denominator, she thought grimly; that was all it was. A chemical response which made no difference to Nick's determination to live as he chose.

She pounded her pillow with her fists. 'I hate him,' she said aloud, her voice wild, her green eyes wet, the dark lashes sticking together in little spikes, then laughed at herself for talking to an empty room. She remembered what Andrew had said to her: fend him off, while you shut out other men too, and you'll end up climbing the walls. Was she going out of her mind? she thought, her mouth wry.

Andrew was right. She could not go on indefinitely with this endless aching need inside her. Nick's love-making had shown her only too clearly that her desire for him was driving her insane. He had grinned when she told him that there had been no other man in the past year, but it was no laughing matter. He had aroused her during their brief marriage, and the needs she was now aware of were eating at her insides.

She sat up on the bed, her face sombre.

What on earth was she going to do about it?

CHAPTER NINE

WHEN Claire returned to London after her brief visit to the cottage in Suffolk, she was aware that she had not resolved her problem. She had spent sleepless nights turning it over and over in her mind, but she had never come to any conclusion. Her stepfather, aware of her mental turmoil, had been quietly withdrawn, leaving her to walk along the beach or wander around the fields, alone, worrying over the alternatives presented to her, unable to decide what to do.

The weather during her visit had been stormy and cold. Across the grey sea the wind blew wildly, cutting through her parka, making her shiver and blowing bright colour into her cheeks. The sky was whipped into a dark chaos, the clouds like heaving leaden waves, streaming before the ruthless wind, bringing showers of cold rain at intervals.

When she walked into the office after her return, Andrew gave her a swift, all-seeing glance and smiled, satisfied. 'You look better,' he told her, surprising her, since she felt the same.

Later she caught sight of her reflection in the cloak-room mirror and realised that the long, windblown walks along the coast had given her a healthy glow which belied the look of strain in her green eyes.

She plunged herself back into her work with a driving need to forget everything else. Andrew had to visit some hotels in the Midlands, and suggested she accompany him. After a brief pause for thought, she agreed, her eyes thoughtful.

The week they spent driving around the Midlands, from hotel to hotel, was in complete contrast to their visit to Keravi. The weather was appalling. Rain washed over the windscreen, obscuring the road. The temperature was permanently low. Claire was grateful, in the evenings, for the central heating which the hotels offered, her bones aching with the chill which the weather inflicted. Andrew noticed her shivering one evening, hunched in a cardigan beside the hotel radiator, and grimaced at her. 'Rotten weather,' he muttered. 'I'm sorry I asked you to come. If I'd known what it would be like I would have left you in London.'

'I'm fine,' she said lightly. 'Anyway, you would never have managed without secretarial help.' He had kept her hard at work every day. She had been through two notebooks already, filling them with his terse, sharp-eyed comments. Andrew needed someone permanently trailing behind him to pick up his decisions and put them down in black and white. He saw everything and could make immediate decisions, but he needed backing.

'You're the best secretary I've ever had,' he told her, taking her by surprise, not because she did not know he valued her work but because it was rare for him to make such flattering comparisons. Andrew paid her well and had always seemed to imagine that that was the end of it.

She smiled at him, her oval face a little pinched with cold. 'Thank you. You're a good boss to work for.' It was true. He was scrupulously fair, generous and calm-tempered. She had worked for men far less kind, far

less thoughtful and far more difficult to get on with—
and one or two had had wandering hands, too, which
had made it impossible to feel easy in their company.
Andrew had never shown signs of that, thank God.

He grinned now. 'A mutual admiration society,' he
murmured lightly. 'At least we've finished with work
now. We could drive home tomorrow morning. I was
going to call in at another place, but that can wait. It
isn't urgent. And I'm sick of this rain.'

Claire was relieved. London was a welcoming place
in the rain—the dull, cold feeling of these Midland
towns seemed absent in the capital, perhaps because it
was home to her now, perhaps because even in the
middle of the night or the depths of winter, London
seems so alive. There was something so depressing
about the chill, grey landscape as they drove back
south. The potbanks loomed like miniature volcanoes
against the leaden sky. The rows of dark little houses,
the gritty feel of the air, intensified somehow by the
sleeting rain, seemed to linger on the mind's eye
dismally.

'I'll drop you at your place,' said Andrew, staring
ahead into the busy London traffic. 'Doing anything
tonight? I thought we might cheer ourselves up after
the last few days by having dinner somewhere special.'

She was taken aback. It was the first time he had ever
seriously asked her to go out with him, and for a
moment it was on the tip of her tongue to reject his
invitation, very politely, but firmly enough to make
sure he never did so again.

Then she thought of her cold, empty apartment, and
her endless spiral of thoughts of Nick, and said quickly,
'Thank you. I'd like that.'

He looked at her sideways, sharply, and she knew he had anticipated a refusal. 'Good,' he said, before she had time to reconsider. 'I'll pick you up at seven.'

After he had dropped her at her apartment she was swamped with doubts as to the wisdom of what she was doing. The last thing she wanted was to get involved in a dead-end relationship with another man—because she knew perfectly well that all other men could mean nothing to her. But she had done it now. She had accepted Andrew's invitation.

She flicked through her wardrobe, grimacing, looking for a dress which would look presentable enough for dinner somewhere special without giving Andrew any unacceptable ideas. In the end she chose a very simple dress in a green shade which almost matched the colour of her eyes—the stiff silken material of the skirt swished as she moved, yet the bodice curved softly over her figure, outlining the graceful shape of her body. It had no frills, no exaggerated line to mar the cool effect of it. She eyed herself with satisfaction, knowing she looked both attractive and slightly aloof at the same time.

When Andrew arrived he gave her a long glance, a smile hovering around his mouth. 'I can practically read the label,' he said, his eyes amused.

She was puzzled for a moment. 'The label?' The dress did look expensive, she knew, but like all her clothes it was the result of careful buying rather than expense. She had bought it in a small boutique in Chelsea, in fact, during a sale.

'Hands off,' Andrew said a little mockingly, and she laughed, a slight flush on her face.

'Well, I am married,' she pointed out, glad that she

could now be open about it.

'But for how long?' he asked, his brows lifting.

She felt her face stiffen. It was a question which she had asked herself many times in the past week, but she had no wish to discuss it with him.

'Where are we dining?' she asked.

He grimaced. 'You have a gift for evading answering which is nothing short of brilliant,' he returned. 'O.K., we don't discuss your marriage. We're dining at Pellerino's—I've booked a table for eight, so we'll have plenty of time for a drink first. They have a floor show at ten which is worth seeing, I'm told.'

When they walked into the bar at Pellerino's it was already half full. While they sipped their drinks, they studied the menu and discussed the food at length. Andrew's professional interest in the subject meant that he was never ready merely to choose a meal by appetite —he liked to gauge the strengths and weaknesses of other hotels and restaurants, he liked to have a mental idea of which restaurant offered which course at its best. So now he frowned and chewed his lip, discarding various alternatives, before he finally settled, for both of them, upon a choice.

Claire watched him with amusement, allowing him to choose for her, knowing that to refuse would only mean that he would become sulky. He eyed the furnishings, scrutinising them with eagle eyes.

'Not bad,' he muttered to her. 'A little too bright for my taste, but not bad.' He had theories about the décor in a bar—he believed the customer preferred a discreet luxury to over-glossy, intrusive décor.

Didn't he ever get tired of thinking about work? she wondered, her eyes smiling.

At that moment his eyes flicked back to her, catching the smile. 'What's funny?' he asked at once, his own mouth quizzical.

'Nothing,' she said. Nothing that he would have found in the least amusing, anyway. Andrew had little sense of humour where his work was concerned. His rapid rise in the business had been fuelled by his constant, unremitting absorption in work.

He lifted a hand to stroke the smooth curve of her satiny cheek. 'No?' he enquired, staring into her eyes, his head leaned towards her with a faint smile.

At that instant she became aware of a movement behind them and vaguely turned her black head. Her unwary eyes looked straight into Nick's harsh, frowning face and a wash of bright colour swept up her face to her hairline. Her lips trembled with the shock and delight of seeing him, her heart thudded violently.

Andrew had turned too, his hand still lying along her jawbone. She felt the fingers stiffen as he glanced from Nick to Philippa, who was standing at his side.

There was a brief silence which seemed to her to be tight with violence.

Then Andrew stood up, smiling tautly. 'Imagine meeting you here,' he said.

'Imagine,' Nick drawled, and the blue eyes were narrowed with hostility.

'You got away safely, then,' Andrew pressed on, undeterred by Nick's cold tone.

'As you see . . .' Nick was not giving an inch. There was ice in the cool tone, ice in the blue eyes. He flicked a look at Claire and she winced from the impact of it.

'We were very worried about you,' Andrew said brightly.

'I'm sure you were,' murmured Nick, deliberately implying the opposite, and again the blue eyes lashed at Claire. She sat like a stone statue, looking at him, feeding the bitter longings of the past days, hating and loving, aware of the increased tempo of her heartbeat and the bitter-sweet ache of pleasure just this sight of him was beginning deep inside her body.

'Have a drink with us,' Andrew invited, only then including Philippa in his glance. He waved a hand at the table. 'Just the two of you tonight?' There was faint hardness in his voice now.

Philippa took the seat beside Claire and looked at her as she sat down. She was wearing pants again, but black velvet ones this time, which tightly hugged her slim body, emphasising every curve. Her top was a loose white silk blouse whose drawstring held it down to her hips, the stiff tailored lapels folded back to reveal her rounded breasts. She looked very sexy, Claire thought bitterly, and like this she gave no one the impression of being a boy. Her sex was only too obvious and only too appealing.

'How long have you been back in England?' she asked her huskily.

'We arrived this morning,' said Philippa.

'I expect you were glad to see the back of Keravi,' Claire said, fiddling with the low tray of cheese straws and peanuts which occupied the middle of the table.

'We weren't sorry,' Philippa answered, smiling at her.

'Was it very bad?' asked Claire, her voice lowering.

'No worse than usual,' Philippa shrugged. The golden eyes surveyed Claire thoughtfully. 'We get used to situations like that, you know. It isn't the first time for us.'

'No,' Claire agreed, swallowing. They did it all the time. It was just in the day's work for them. She felt deeply depressed. Not for the first time, she wished she could hate Philippa. Nick had brought her here to-night; they obviously saw each other often outside their work. The intimacy between them spread beyond the daily routine to more social occasions, after all. Nick had said there had been nobody else for him during their separation, but if she divorced him how long would it be before Philippa took her place?

She was just the sort of girl for Nick—level-headed, brave, clever, a professional in his lunatic world of death and daily risk.

The drinks arrived and Andrew lifted his glass, his mouth wry. 'A toast, then—to the end of an adventure . . .'

Philippa looked at him. 'We were all very impressed by the way you got Nick and Claire out of that room,' she said.

'I had a great time,' he shrugged.

'You were obviously cut out for that sort of life,' Philippa murmured. 'You should have gone into the army.'

He laughed. 'Not enough scope,' he said. 'I enjoy my present job, anyway. I'm good at it and that's half the battle.'

It was true. Andrew enjoyed organising. He liked to run things. He wasn't a man to sit idly by and see anything which needed a controlling hand without wading in and sorting it out, by force if necessary.

Claire could feel Nick's eyes moving over her, although he had shielded those brilliant blue eyes with his lowered lashes. She did not look at him, concentrating instead on Philippa, who was talking lightly, sharing her attention between Andrew and herself, sketching in for them the events which had followed their departure, glossing over the things which she knew would cause shock or dismay, dwelling instead upon several amusing incidents which had happened to the team.

'None of you got hurt?' Claire asked at one point.

The golden eyes flashed to her. 'None of us,' Philippa said quite gently. 'We're quite good at self-protection, you know.'

'Yes,' Claire said huskily, looking down.

The waiter materialised and announced that their table was free. Andrew glanced from Nick to Philippa. 'I suppose you wouldn't like to join us?' His voice was brusque, yet held a tinge of uncertainty, and his eyes lingered on Philippa's face as he waited for an answer.

She looked at Nick, her features expressionless.

He flickered a look at her, his brows lifted, then glanced past her at Claire's averted profile. She was running a finger around the rim of her glass, her head bent, the smooth white curve of her neck shadowed by her black hair.

'Why not?' Nick said coolly, watching as Claire half turned to look at him quickly.

Their eyes met, and a pain shot through her, her eyes fell away from his, afraid she would reveal too much by her expression. She had waited numbly for his answer. Now she was half dreading, half longing for the sweetness of being with him for several hours.

Andrew took charge of the evening with all his usual efficiency, insisting that they would wait until Nick and Philippa had ordered their main course and ordering the waiter to bring another round of drinks while they waited for the kitchen to deal with the change in plans. 'If you have the same first course as we've ordered it will make it simpler,' he pointed out. Nick's mouth compressed but he nodded. Since the ordered first course was cold, it would obviously make it easier. The waiter sped away, looking irritated, and they waited uneasily while the necessary shift was made, then walked through to the dining-room and sat down.

Philippa continued to make polite conversation as they ate the first course, but the strain of the atmosphere was telling on her too as she left longer and longer spaces between her remarks, glancing from Nick to Andrew with a wry twitch at her mouth.

Suddenly Andrew began to talk about their tour of the Midlands, graphically describing some of the back-stairs horrors he had found. 'A filthy cockroach in the kitchen,' he said, his strong face rigid with distaste 'Any hint of that getting out and the place would empty like a sinking boat . . . as soon as the decorators can get in there we'll have to have the whole place done over.'

'And did you enjoy your trip to the Midlands?' Nick asked Claire silkily, the blue eyes biting.

It was the first time he had spoken to her directly She started, her green eyes opening wide, vulnerable and filled with dazed emotion.

'I . . .' To her horror, her voice seemed to freeze, the words refusing to emerge, and a slow wave of hot colour swept up her skin.

She saw Nick's nostrils flare, a white line grow around the hard mouth, the bitter brilliance of his eyes increase, and she knew with a sinking heart that he had taken her reaction for some hint of guilt. His dark head turned slowly to focus a harsh stare upon Andrew, who lowered his head to his plate again, dismaying her.

Philippa took a long swallow of wine and said brightly, 'Perhaps it might interest you both to come and look around the studios some time.'

Andrew lifted his head again and stared at her, his brown eyes glinting. 'We'd be fascinated,' he said. 'Wouldn't we, Claire?'

The deliberate pairing of their names made Claire feel sick. She wished miserably that she had refused his invitation to dinner. It had been a catastrophic error.

The waiter removed their plates and began to serve the main course. Philippa took some more wine, then very brightly, in a tone now faintly hectic with assumed gaiety, began to talk about politics. It was, as she knew very well by now, the red rag to Andrew's bull, and Claire could sense her waving it deliberately, her golden eyes challenging him.

Andrew lowered his head as if about to charge and within five minutes they were at it hammer and tongs, their voices sharp, their faces flushed and intent. The silence between the other two no longer mattered. Claire sipped her wine and toyed with her food, grateful to Philippa, guessing that she had been avoiding that very topic until now but had thrown caution to the winds in an attempt to keep them off more dangerous subjects.

The rest of the meal passed for Claire in a haze. She ate and drank without any idea of what was passing her lips, conscious all the time of Nick's grim, brooding presence on the other side of her, although he never once seemed to glance at her.

She was surprised at some stage to realise that the furious battle between Andrew and Philippa had altered its dimension somehow. Andrew was laughing, his brown eyes glinting, and Philippa was smiling back at him quite naturally. Claire had long ago lost the thread of their argument, but now she began to listen again and found that, in the circular motion of their talk, they had come back to the subject of Keravi again, and were laughing over some incident which had happened on the morning Philippa rescued Andrew from his room.

'All the same,' Andrew said, 'I owe you my life.'

'Rubbish,' retorted Philippa, pushing his thanks away brusquely. 'You have too much sense to have got killed. You would have caught on to what was happening.'

'I might have done,' he agreed. 'But it might have been too late. So thanks, anyway.'

They both transferred their attention to their coffee simultaneously just as the floor show began. The jazz trio who opened the evening were well worth listening to, although Claire could have wished they made less noise, since her head was beginning to ache. Andrew moved his chair back a little, leaning back, his shoulder close to her own, smoking a cigar. Flickering a glance towards Nick, she saw him watching them, that bitter pull at his hard mouth. The blue eyes flashed over her icily and were withdrawn. Suddenly she knew she could not bear his proximity a second longer.

Leaning forward, she whispered to Andrew, 'I'm sorry, I've got a headache. Do you mind if I leave early? I'll take a taxi home.'

His face fell. 'I'll take you home,' he said reluctantly, turning to rise.

Before she could move, Nick was on his feet, his hand

on her wrist. 'I'll take her,' he said. 'I've got to get an early night myself. I have an editing session in the morning. Can you see Pippa home?'

Andrew sank back into his chair. 'Delighted,' he said casually. 'Take the day off tomorrow, Claire. You're probably tired after our Midlands trip.'

Philippa smiled at her. 'Nice to meet you again, Claire. I hope I'll see you again soon.'

She was white and shivering, as though she had caught a chill during her trip to the Midlands, but somehow she managed a polite smile to them both, murmuring something totally inaudible as she allowed Nick to propel her away from them out of the restaurant.

'My car's parked round the corner,' he said, his hand dropping away from her as they walked out into the night. It had stopped raining and the air was cool and fresh. The street lamps shone in dazzling reflection on the wet pavements. The sky arched overhead in clear dark blue.

Nick unlocked his car and she slid into the passenger seat. He closed the door and walked round to get into the driver's seat. They had not said one word during the moments since they left the others. Claire wondered if he meant to maintain this frozen silence until he left her, and tried desperately to think of something to say to him, but failed. She could not have borne to make polite small talk to him, and anything else was too painful.

He got behind the wheel and laid his hands on it, staring ahead, his profile diamond sharp against the darkness. She glanced at him nervously, wondering what was going through his mind.

'M—my address . . .' she began, but he broke into the sentence brusquely.

'I know.'

She bit her lower lip. Of course he knew. He had read her letters to her father. Why was he sitting there? Why didn't he start the car? Was he about to tell her he was starting divorce proceedings?

A shiver ran over her body and she wrapped her arms around herself, cursing the fact that she had not brought a coat with her. Andrew, with typical efficiency, had had an umbrella with which to shield her from the downpour as they walked from his parked car to the restaurant.

Nick glanced sideways and made an irritated sound. 'You're frozen,' he snapped, then leaned over the back of the car, the movement causing his hard body to brush against her. Producing a short suede car coat from the back seat, he pushed it at her. 'Put this on.'

'What about you?' she asked huskily.

'I'm warm enough,' he muttered. She ran her eyes over the dark grey suit he was wearing and realised that he was undoubtedly warmer dressed than she was, so she slid her arms into the fur-lined coat and snuggled down inside it, deeply conscious of the fact that it was his, that it already held the constant imprint of his body, the suede faintly lined at elbow and shoulder from his wear of it.

'How bad is your headache?' he asked abruptly, without looking at her.

'It . . . was the jazz music,' she said nervously. 'All that noise.'

'Does it still ache?' he asked, his voice irritated.

'No,' she admitted, knowing that she had only really

wanted to get away from the difficult atmosphere around the table.

He started the engine then and drew slowly away, still staring ahead. Turning into the flow of traffic he said quietly, 'We've got to talk, Claire. Your place or mine?'

Her heart missed a beat. She looked at him, passing a tongue over her dry lips. He seemed so distant and remote, an unreachable stranger, and she was deeply afraid of what he was going to say to her.

When she didn't answer Nick turned his head, the dark hair falling away from that hard profile, and the brilliant eyes flashed at her.

'Protest all you like, Claire,' he said between tight lips. 'This time I'm taking you somewhere where bloody Andrew can't interrupt, and we're going to talk this thing out.'

CHAPTER TEN

THEY drove down towards the river, through quiet dark streets whose street lamps shed ineffectual pools of light on the rainy pavements, passing a few late-night wanderers who were sauntering along, their voices hushed by the surrounding silence of the city. Emerging into the flow of traffic along the Embankment, the car slowed for a while, then put on speed. Claire stared blankly at the high wall shielding the dark current of the Thames from view. On the south side of the river the brilliant lights ate into the tossed sky. The slow curve of the Thames was edged with the soft shapes of office buildings, their varied heights and forms like children's building blocks, only the spires and domes giving the skyscape that special glamour. Oddly she remembered the first time she saw the city. She had walked over Westminster Bridge in the cool brightness of a March morning, remembering Wordsworth's sonnet, marvelling that two centuries had not diminished its validity. Tonight, in her highly charged frame of mind, the city wore a mantle of beauty every inch as striking, and she sighed.

Nick shot her a sideways look. 'Still cold?'

'No,' she said huskily, huddling deeper into the fur-lined warmth of his coat as if she were held safely in his arms.

He turned up a side street in Chelsea, purring along the wet road until he parked outside a tall, narrow house. She looked up at it, her mouth denting. 'Your apartment?'

'My apartment,' he agreed.

She was suddenly tense, afraid of what he would say or do once they were alone. Licking dry lips, she said nervously, 'Can't we talk here?'

He laughed harshly. 'No, we damned well can't!' Getting out, he came round to open her door, pulling her out with hands which did not even attempt to be gentle.

'Stop bullying me!' she flung in a flurry of anger.

The strong fingers gripped her arm, the lean dark face bent towards her, blue eyes sparking in the light of a street lamp. 'Stop defying me,' he warned. 'I won't put up with it.'

'You won't!' She raised her chin rebelliously, the green eyes fever sharp. 'You seem to forget, you have no rights where I'm concerned any more, Nick.' Not, she thought, since he refused to come home to England with her, although he was wounded.

The hard mouth drew into a bitter line. 'Do as you're told,' he snapped fiercely, pushing her in front of him up the steps of the house. He held her arm while he found his key and let them into the narrow hall, then unlocked the door of his apartment on the ground floor, propelled her inside and followed, closing the door behind them. She stood there like a recalcitrant mule, her slender figure erect, while he switched on the light.

They stood in a small lobby from which several doors led. Nick opened one, flicked on the switch and lifted his coat from her as if she were a difficult child. 'I'll put the electric fire on,' he said, moving past her to do so.

Curiously Claire glanced around the room. It had the

same tidy, empty appearance of his previous apartment. It was a shell, not a home.

'Sit down,' he ordered, flickering a glance over her.

She reluctantly obeyed, sinking into a deep chintz-covered armchair near the glowing fire. Nick leaned on the wall, staring down at her. She let her eyes continue to travel around the room. There was a line of books on a shelf, a single oil painting over the fireplace—she stared at it with a start, recognising the Suffolk coast-line, the empty grey sea, the white-winged gulls in specks above it, the stormy wind driven sky. Nick's glance followed hers and his mouth moved wryly.

'Like it?'

'Yes,' she said, still staring at it. 'When did you buy it?'

'Last time I was down at the cottage,' he said. 'I drove Dad over to Ipswich to see your aunt and I saw that in a gallery, so I went in and got it.'

Claire's heart missed a beat. It was the only thing in the room which was personal. It was a shred of com-mitment. It tethered him, whether he knew it or not, and it meant that something pulled him back to Eng-land, to Suffolk, to her. I must be crazy to find that so moving, she thought in sickening misery. In his pre-vious apartment there had been nothing that could not have vanished without his noticing. He had had no pos-sessions, a man who frequently departed without notice, leaving everything behind, and that had been a significant part of her anger towards him. She had never really believed he felt committed to her. He had been as free as one of those gulls—a wanderer who might any day take off and never return.

'Would you like some coffee?' he asked abruptly,

breaking into her silence.

She looked at him. 'Thank you.'

'Come and see my kitchen,' he invited, not yet moving.

She stood up slowly, suddenly sensing that he wanted her to go with him in case she walked out while he was making the coffee.

The kitchen was as tidy and featureless as the sitting-room. Nick moved around, making coffee, while she stood and watched him, wondering how he could bear this sort of life. Her own place, even after this short year, was marked with her own personality. She had ornaments and flowers everywhere, a few cheap reproductions of favourite pictures, a pile of records and a second-hand stereo player which she had bought in a junk shop in a mad mood. Nick's apartment was untouched by his presence. If he died tomorrow she would never be hurt by anything here—it bore no reminding brand. Except for that picture of Suffolk.

They carried the coffee into the sitting-room. He placed a coffee table in front of the low couch and jerked a hand towards it, watching as she put down the tray. Claire went to move back to her chair, but his fingers caught her wrist. 'No, you don't!' he muttered between his teeth.

'Stop it, Nick,' she snapped, glaring at him.

'Sit down,' he commanded, pushing her towards the couch.

She sat, rebelliously, keeping a distance between them as he joined her. Leaning forward, she poured the coffee, added sugar to his and handed it to him.

He placed it on the table and leaned back, folding his arms. The lean, dark features were blank as he watched her. 'First things first,' he said. 'Andrew Knight . . . what's the real situation, Claire?'

'We've already been over that,' she said, staring into her cup, watching the marbled swirl of the cream as it sank into the liquid.

'That was before he risked his life to get you safely out of Keravi,' he said in a cool voice.

'Andrew is very brave,' she said. 'And he had a strong sense of responsibility.'

Nick laughed coldly. 'Tell me again he doesn't want you.'

She looked up at that. 'I've no idea,' she said frankly. At one time she had been sure Andrew didn't give a damn for her, but now she had no real idea at all. He was a difficult man to read.

Nick's mouth compressed. 'All right, we'll come at it by another route,' he said. 'Has he kissed you?'

She flushed, looking away.

'I see,' said Nick, anger pulsing in his voice even though the words were uttered in a staccato fashion.

'Don't read too much into that,' she said quietly. 'Andrew has a lot of women. I've worked for him for a year. They come and go and I don't think any of them has meant that much to him. Some of them used to give me jealous glares, but there was never anything between Andrew and myself.'

'Until now?'

The question was unanswerable. She had no inkling. Andrew's behaviour had puzzled her a good deal lately. She sighed. 'Even so, that has nothing to do with us.'

'No?' Nick sounded grim.

The green eyes flared angrily at him. 'No,' she insisted. 'Our marriage concerns nobody but ourselves, and the fact remains that you feel free to walk out on me any time you choose . . .'

'Before we discuss our marriage I want to get it straight about the way you feel towards your boss,' Nick said abruptly.

'I've told you a dozen times . . . I like him, nothing more.'

'Yet when you thought he was risking his life for you, you went as white as a sheet and you were shaking,' he said tersely.

'I hate violence,' she said. 'I'm a coward. It would have been the same if it had been Wazi or Philippa out there with a rifle. I would have been just as scared for them, just as guilty that they were risking their lives for me.'

He studied her intently. 'That's all?'

'That's all,' she agreed.

'And on the beach?' Nick asked drily. 'You wouldn't let me lay a finger on you, but when I looked back, you were in his arms, and you were clinging to him.'

She flushed. 'Yes.' She remembered the agony of those moments as if it had been yesterday and her skin whitened with the memory. Huskily she said, 'I'd just said goodbye to you and I thought it might be for ever.'

'Yet you wouldn't kiss me,' he shot back bitterly.

She bent her head. 'I know. That was why I was crying. I wanted to so badly, but I was angry and hurt . . . when you'd gone I felt as if I were bleeding to death.'

'You were!' Violence burnt in his voice. 'God, I still don't know how I walked away from you. When I looked back and saw you in his arms I almost came back and shot him with that damned rifle.'

She gave a hysterical crack of laughter. 'How ungrateful of you, Nick!'

He wasn't amused, the brilliant blue eyes searing. 'You expect me to be grateful to him? For waltzing off with you under my very nose? I hate the bastard!'

'He got us out of there . . .' she began.

'He's in love with you. You pretend not to see it, but maybe you've never noticed the way he looks at you. He wants you, Claire.'

'If he does, he's never said or done anything to make it clear to me,' she said, although that wasn't strictly true. Andrew had been making a few elementary passes towards her, but he had never pressed the issue, and she still wasn't sure whether he was serious or just playing the usual game of light flirtation.

'Tonight he was touching you when we arrived,' Nick muttered, staring at her.

Claire blushed. 'Only lightly . . . it didn't mean a thing.'

'It meant this,' said Nick, moving suddenly, his hand gripping her soft chin, turning her face towards him. 'It meant I wanted to choke the smile off his face . . .'

The touch of the long fingers was sending a pulsing heat around her body. She looked at him helplessly, her eyes slowly dropping to the hard mouth.

There was a silence. Nick leaned forward and she instinctively drew nearer, her eyes riveted on his lips. He muttered something under his breath and suddenly pulled away, releasing her.

'That's the easy way out,' he said in a shaken voice. 'We're both well aware that we click, but there's a lot to talk about first, Claire. What are we going to do about our marriage? I can't go on like this for any longer.'

She sighed, deeply shaken too. 'Nothing has changed, though, has it? You have no intention of giving way, yet you expect me to.'

He stood up and swung away, leaning against the fireplace, his back to her. 'Damn you,' he muttered under his breath. 'I'm not grovelling, Claire.'

No, she thought. You wouldn't give an inch, but you want me to give everything. 'If you loved me,' she said miserably, 'you wouldn't want to put me through that sort of hell every time you went away. You ask too much, Nick. Despise me if you like, but I know it would kill me after a little while.'

'You haven't even tried,' he said, his back still towards her. His voice sounded odd, thick, impeded.

She stared at the lean body, wondering if it was her imagination that he was trembling. A peculiar weakness invaded her. It couldn't be possible that he was suffering, that he was hiding weakness from her? Slowly she stood up and saw his body tense.

She moved and he swung round. 'Claire, don't go.'

The familiar voice was suddenly unfamiliar, shaking, filled with pleading. She stared at his pale face, the wet glitter of the blue eyes.

'Oh, Nick!' she groaned, and was in his arms a second later, his hands holding her fiercely, possessively.

'I love you,' he said in that husky, shaken voice, his mouth moving against her throat. 'Don't leave me.'

She wound her arms around his waist, clinging to him, her hands stroking over his back, comforting him. 'I won't,' she promised. 'I swear I won't.'

She had resisted his strength, his desire, his insistence, but she found she was helpless against his weakness. It was the first time she had ever seen him other than unyielding, and she could not bear it.

Against her, she felt a sigh drain him. The long fingers lifted her chin and she looked into his eyes. He flushed, smiling wryly at her. 'I'm crazy about you, Claire.' It sounded like a confession, an unwilling admission. 'I always have been, from the first day—the last year has been hell.'

She watched his mouth moving as he spoke, the outline taut. Putting a finger against it, she smiled into his eyes. 'I love you too,' she told him. 'And I suppose I've always known I had to take you as you were, however much it was going to hurt.'

'It won't be as bad as it used to be,' he promised, quickly. 'This new job is different. I can't say there won't be times when I'm sent abroad to dangerous places, but most of the year I'll be in England.'

Claire was limp with relief, her hands moving softly through the dark hair now, although she knew she would have stayed anyway. Nick had defeated her, not by a demonstration of power, but more subtly, by allowing her to defeat him, knowing, perhaps that she could never accept such a victory. For both their sakes, he had to win. She could not have borne to have it any other way.

He drew her back down on to the couch, loosening her black hair with tender fingers, drawing the fine glinting strands of it through his hands. 'We'll buy a house,' he said. 'It will have to be within driving distance of London, but we could get one halfway between here and Suffolk, then we could pop down to see your father at weekends.'

'That would be nice,' she said, barely listening, although one part of her mind took in the words with a lift of the heart, because she thought that she could make him a home, a place he would find it hard to leave. The other nine tenths of her mind was intent on tracing the strong, lean features which, at last, she could bear to look at fully, knowing that they would not be parted again.

Nick's hand curved round her cheek, the warmth of his palm lying softly against her warm skin. 'I'll make you happy,' he promised huskily.

She watched his mouth, her heart beginning to beat wildly. 'Make me happy now,' she whispered unsteadily.

He drew a long breath. 'Gladly,' he said, his voice very deep, then he lifted her into his arms and carried her into the bedroom. The year apart had done one thing, she thought, lying in his arms. It had given the sharp edge of frustrated necessity to their passion. It had always been fantastic between them, but now Nick was shuddering as his hands moved over her, and her own heart was beating so fast she was almost frightened.

His lips slid hungrily over her bare shoulders, his hands lifting her closer. 'Darling,' he muttered. 'Claire, my love . . .'

She had a brief memory of their wedding night; her own nervous excitement, Nick's calming and expert lovemaking. He had not been driven by the same need then, she realised. He had loved her, wanted her, but there was a world of difference between that night and this—tonight she suddenly knew he would promise her almost anything. Before their marriage, he had always been the master of the situation between them. He had made the rules. She had been swept off her feet, too crazy about him to question any of his decisions. She thought of her easy acceptance of his decision that they should have no children for a few years. She had wanted to be alone with him, then—now she wondered if she should have had a child, after all. It might have made everything easier.

Nick looked down at her, suddenly aware that she was not entirely with him. A frown etched itself between his dark brows. 'What's wrong?' he asked anxiously.

She laid her cheek against his shoulder, brushing his skin with her lips. 'Not a thing, dearest,' she whispered. 'But . . .'

'But what?' he asked quickly.

'I want a child,' she said, her eyes smiling at him. 'I know we said no children for a few years, but I want your child and I don't think I could bear to wait.'

There was a brief silence, then he grinned quizzically. 'First things first, sweetheart,' he teased. 'There's no rush to make a decision like that, is there?'

'You do want a child, though?' she asked.

'Your child? Yes,' he said, his face sober. 'Yes, I want you to have a child.' A wry light came into the blue eyes. 'A home, a child . . . are you going to enjoy weaving your silken little ropes around me, Claire?'

'Our home, our child,' she pointed out, smiling.

'Tomorrow,' Nick said urgently, his strong fingers pulling her closer. 'I've other things on my mind just now and I don't want you thinking of anything but me.'

Her lashes fluttered down as his head bent towards her, her hands clinging to his shoulders as her body arched against him in pliant submission. 'This time,' he muttered as he conquered her mouth, 'there will be no interruptions, I promise you . . .'

The rapid hammering of her heart sent the blood singing in her ears. She ran her trembling hands down his back, her mouth parted under his, responding fully to the slow caress of the hands which were stroking over her. Desire seemed to accelerate within both of them at a pace which sent her senses wild. Nick pressed her down on the bed, exploring the warm skin of her throat with his mouth, groaning inaudibly against her.

The eruption of the telephone startled them both into immobility. Nick swore under his breath. The shrill sound went on and on.

'You'll have to answer it,' she said at last, wearily.

'Damn them,' he muttered. 'I will not.'

'It may be urgent,' she said, remembering those other calls which had dragged him from her long ago.

'Let them find someone else,' he muttered, his body tense against her.

The sound stopped with a suddenness that was almost as startling as when it began. Nick lay still for a second, breathing heavily, then he laughed wryly. 'The first cock crew,' he said with an ambiguity which puzzled her for a moment, until she tracked the reference down. 'You'll have me tied to an office desk yet,' he added with faint grimness.

'Nick?' She was perturbed by the sound of his voice. Was he angry even though it had been his own decision to ignore the phone?

'Shut up,' he said roughly. 'I want you like hell, and nothing in this world is going to stop me having you tonight.'

Claire gasped as his body returned to her, with a violence which was electrifying, but her own need rose to meet his demands, the wild passion between them driving everything but him from her mind.

Nick slept like the dead when she awoke next morning. She slipped out of the bed, leaving him asleep, dressed quietly in the tiny bathroom and went into the kitchen to make some coffee. Examining the contents of the kitchen she grimaced. He had almost nothing in stock. What did he live on? She heard a movement from the bedroom and took him a cup of coffee, finding him out of the bed, his face tense. He relaxed as she came into the room, and she guessed that he had been afraid he would find her gone.

She kissed him lingeringly, feeling the quickening beat of his heart against her own. 'I'll have to do some shopping this morning,' she said. 'There's nothing to eat in that kitchen.'

'Who wants to eat?' he asked lazily, holding her with one arm while he sipped his coffee. 'I can think of much more interesting occupations.'

'Talking about occupations,' she said slowly. 'About my job . . .'

His face hardened. 'You're resigning as of now.'

'Nick, that wouldn't be fair to Andrew,' she protested.

'Damn Andrew!' His mouth thinned. 'I won't have you working for him for another day. He can find a replacement.'

'It will be very inconvenient for him!'

'I'm crying,' Nick snapped. The blue eyes glittered at her. 'Claire, promise me you won't go back there.'

She sighed, looking at him wryly. He expected her to throw up her job at a moment's notice, but he would not give up his! His face tightened into a hard mask, but she saw the tinge of pallor creep under his skin, and knew that beneath his fierce determination there pulsed an anxiety he was trying to hide.

'Oh, well, if you insist,' she said, capitulating. She remembered last night, when he had ignored the telephone, and ruefully thought that no victory is unlimited. They each had to learn to compromise. Marriage was an endless lesson in how to give in gracefully, how to accept victory tenderly. The important thing was the basic need for each other, and she no longer doubted that Nick needed her as badly as she needed him.

He relaxed, his smile returning. 'We'll do the shopping together,' he suggested. 'You can move your things this afternoon. I'll settle with your landlord, then this weekend we'll start house-hunting, shall we?'

'Yes, darling,' she said. He kissed her and went into the bathroom. She heard the bath water running as she began to make a shopping list. There was a peculiar sweetness in beginning to build a life with him. She looked around the tidy, empty room. She would manage to make it into a home until they found a house of their own. There was nothing in it now which could bring Nick hurrying back from the other side of the world, but in a few days she could turn it into something which would haunt his sleep and pull him back to her wherever he was.

The doorbell went. Sighing, she opened it and looked in surprise at Philippa and Andrew. Philippa's golden eyes lit with amusement.

'Hi. Are visitors permitted? Or would we be intruding?'

Claire laughed and stood back. 'Of course, come in
. . . Nick's having a bath.'

Andrew looked sheepishly at her as he passed into the
sitting-room. Curiously, she wondered why he was
with Philippa, and what had brought them here.
Philippa soon enlightened her.

'Work, I'm afraid,' she said regretfully. 'They rang
me last night. They said Nick wasn't at home.' The
leonine eyes teased lightly. 'I said I had no idea where
he was.'

'Thank you,' Claire said gratefully, then, her throat
closing, 'Where is it this time?'

Philippa gave her a comprehending look, her glance
calming. 'Oh, nothing urgent. Just that they wanted
him to expedite the Keravi film he'd brought back.
They have this weird time scale. Now means yesterday,
and soon means right this minute.'

'Oh.' Claire was weak with relief. She gave Andrew
a worried look. She had to tell him now.

'Nick wants me to stop working right away,' she told
him carefully. 'I'm sorry, Andrew. I'm sure you'll find
a good replacement for me, though.'

'Oh, that's great,' he snapped, looking irritated.
'What am I supposed to do in the meantime? Type my
letters myself?'

'You'll manage,' Philippa told him coolly. 'Don't
fuss, Andrew.'

Claire looked at her in surprise, then at Andrew. That
mulish, belligerent look was back in his face and his
eyes were bright with temper.

'What the hell do you know about it?' he asked
hoarsely.

Claire went into the kitchen and began to make some

more coffee. She heard their voices rising, then suddenly Nick's voice in the bathroom as he loudly broke into song, and guessed that he had heard them, too, and was making fun of them. A grin appeared on her face. At least he was cheerful about Andrew's presence. She had been anxious about his reaction to that.

Philippa walked into the kitchen beside her and gave her a quick smile. 'How are things? Fine?'

Claire laughed. 'Yes, thank you.' She liked the understated question, the tactful phrasing. 'How's Andrew bearing up now?'

Philippa dipped a finger in the sugar bowl and licked the fine silver grains off with a slow movement of her pink tongue, like a lazy cat.

'I'm crazy about the fatheaded idiot,' she said, taking Claire by surprise. The golden eyes lifted briefly, a wry smile on her mouth. 'He's carrying a slight torch for you—I imagine you know that.'

Claire blushed, looking away. 'Well, I . . .'

'Come on,' Philippa said drily. 'He looks at you as if he could eat you, and don't tell me Nick hasn't noticed, because I know damn well he has.'

'There's never been a thing between us,' Claire protested.

'You're what Andrew thinks a woman should look like,' Philippa shrugged. 'Soft, feminine, helpless . . . and I'm just the opposite. I'm not sure I want to put up with the long struggle for him, but I'm just insane enough to let myself do it. I've no illusions as to just what I'd be letting myself in for, but there's something about him that gets me.'

Claire laughed helplessly. 'He's a very tough man—

that's why he's so successful.' They fought about every single thing, though, she thought. Was it ever likely to be worth it for Philippa?

'I'm no soft touch myself,' Philippa said with wry humour.

'No, that's true.' But Claire was still doubtful. There would be no peace in a relationship like that. They would be like two cats tied up in a bag.

Philippa was watching her, the handsome boyish head to one side. 'What are you thinking? You're a very cool lady, do you know that? You say very little and you give little away. I can see why both Nick and Andrew fancy you. Still waters are very alluring.'

'I think Andrew would get bored with me,' Claire said, smiling. Then, on an impulse, 'He finds you attractive—I can tell you that.'

Philippa looked at her dubiously. 'Trying to comfort me, Claire?'

'No, it's the truth,' Claire assured her. 'He was reluctant to admit it, but he said going to bed with you would be like going to bed with a wildcat, and I don't think he found the idea unattractive.'

A slow flush burned along Philippa's face. She gave a low chuckle. 'Did he, indeed? Just imagine!'

Claire laughed back at her. 'I think he had!'

'I can think of better things to do in bed than fight like blazes,' Philippa said rather too forcibly, just as Andrew walked into the room.

She swung her head round, colouring, and he stared at her, the brown eyes narrowed.

'Am I interrupting some cosy female gossip?' he asked sarcastically, glancing at Claire, and something in his expression told her that he supposed them to be discussing her night with Nick. A little smile curved her pink mouth.

'Carry this into the other room for me, will you, Andrew?' she asked softly

He obeyed, but said as he placed it on the coffee table, 'I can't stay, I'm afraid. I've got to drive over to Richmond to pay a lightning call on our hotel there. The chef went crazy last night and slashed about with a hatchet. No injuries to anything but the furniture, thank God, but I have to sort it all out.' He glanced at Philippa. 'If you want that lift to Kew you'll have to skip coffee, too.'

'We only called in to pick you up,' Philippa explained to Claire. 'And to give Nick the message that his editing session has been moved forward to nine-thirty, and he's to get moving with the stuff.'

'I'll tell him,' she promised, then glanced at Andrew. 'Sorry I can't come with you and I apologise about the job. I know it leaves you in the lurch, but Nick needs me.'

He held her eyes for a moment, his face blank. Then he shrugged, his broad shoulders easy. 'As Philippa says, I'll manage.' He paused. 'Be happy, Claire,' he said roughly, turning to go.

Philippa winked at her. 'He's wearing his best stiff upper lip,' she whispered. 'Really, there's a lot of the little boy in him, the fool.'

When they had gone Claire heard Nick whistling in the bedroom. He wandered into the room a moment later and stared at the tray, the four cups, the large pot of coffee, then glanced round the room, his brow lifting.

'Where have they hidden?'

'Gone,' she said. 'Andrew was giving Philippa a lift

to Kew. They couldn't stay. The studio want you to expedite the Keravi film and your editing session is fixed for nine-thirty today.'

'God,' he said grimly. 'So that was why they were ringing last night. Anyone would think they owned me.'

'No,' she said, winding her arms around him. 'I do.'

He laughed, kissing her nose. 'Did you tell Andrew you were leaving right away?'

The casual tone did not deceive her. She looked at him with amusement. 'Yes,' she said.

'What did he say?'

'Do you really want to hear?' she asked drily.

'I wish I could have seen his face,' Nick admitted casually, a glint in his blue eyes. 'How come Pip was with him? Don't tell me they spent the night together?'

'I'm sure not,' she said. 'But Philippa has her eye on him—she admitted as much to me.'

Nick grinned. 'I knew that,' he shrugged. 'I know Pip. I saw the way she looked at him when he wasn't looking at her. That's one relationship I wouldn't lay money on, though. They are definitely not suited.'

Claire sighed. 'I agree. They're worlds apart.'

Nick's eyes were thoughtful. 'All the same, Pip's a very determined huntress, and when she puts on the warpaint she can knock your eyes out. Andrew Knight had better watch out. She'll have his scalp before he knows she's behind him!'

Claire looked at him in disgust. 'Poor Andrew . . . I'm not sure he deserves it.'

'Ah,' Nick said wickedly, 'that's the trouble with women. They can make their little traps so attractive that men actually enjoy getting caught in them.'

She stepped away from him, her green eyes taunting.

'You're not trapped, Nick. You're free,' she said softly, her arms open wide.

'The hell I am,' he said, pulling her fiercely into his embrace, and his mouth bent to take her lips with a hunger that drove everything but themselves from their minds.

Harlequin Presents...

Take these 4 best-selling novels FREE

That's right! FOUR first-rate Harlequin romance novels by four world renowned authors, FREE, as your introduction to the Harlequin Presents Subscription Plan. Be swept along by these FOUR exciting, poignant and sophisticated novels . . . . Travel to the Mediterranean island of Cyprus in **Anne Hampson**'s "Gates of Steel" . . . to Portugal for **Anne Mather**'s "Sweet Revenge" . . . to France and **Violet Winspear**'s "Devil in a Silver Room" . . . and the sprawling state of Texas for **Janet Dailey**'s "No Quarter Asked."

Join the millions of avid Harlequin readers all over the world who delight in the magic of a really exciting novel. SIX great NEW titles published EACH MONTH! Each month you will get to know exciting, interesting, true-to-life people . . . . You'll be swept to distant lands you've dreamed of visiting . . . . Intrigue, adventure, romance, and the destiny of many lives will thrill you through each Harlequin Presents novel.

FREE Gift Certificate
and subscription reservation

Mail this coupon today!

In U.S.A.:
Harlequin Reader Service
MPO Box 707
Niagara Falls, NY 14302

In Canada:
Harlequin Reader Service
649 Ontario Street
Stratford, Ontario
N5A 6W4

Harlequin Reader Service:

Please send me my 4 Harlequin Presents books free. Also, reserve a subscription to the 6 new Harlequin Presents novels published each month. Each month I will receive 6 new Presents novels at the low price of $1.50 each [*Total - $9.00 per month*]. There are no shipping and handling or any other hidden charges. I am free to cancel at any time, but even if I do, these first 4 books are still mine to keep absolutely FREE without any obligation.

NAME _____ (PLEASE PRINT)

ADDRESS _____

CITY _____ STATE / PROV. _____ ZIP / POSTAL CODE

Offer expires February 28, 1981
Offer not valid to present subscribers

08374

Prices subject to change without notice.